"You are beautiful," he murmured.

And God help her,

She slipped her arm ~~~~~~~~~~~~~~~~~~~~~~~~~~~~ er,
a little horrified that ~~~~~~~~~~~~~~~~~~~~~~~~~~~~.
But it felt good that ~~~~~~~~~~~~~~~~~~~~~~~~~~~ vas
beautiful and wante~~~~~~~~~~~~~~~~~~~~~~~~~~~ was
enjoying his company. When the song ended, they kept
dancing by silent agreement, moving even more slowly as
the singers took on a Sade song, "Lover's Rock."

Their hips swayed together. Flutters of arousal moved
through Diana's belly, made her skin tingle wherever it
touched his. She knew she should be worried, that she
should move away from him and regain control of herself,
but it felt too good. His touch. The music. The desire
winding around them like a silken ribbon.

The song ended, and Marcus slid his hands around her
waist, pressed his mouth to her forehead.

"I want to kiss you," he murmured.

She trembled at the urgency in his voice. Her hands
tightened for a moment on his shoulders. Her body was
hot with the need for that kiss. "Not here," she said, not
knowing how she would react to his touch in front of all
those people.

He pulled back, took her hand and drew her through
the thin crowd of dancers. Down a quiet, wood-paneled
hallway. The smell of cigars, wood smoke. Emptiness.
He pressed her against the wall, hips against hers, hands
planted on either side of her head. His mouth swooped
down, lightly touching hers and asking permission.

Books by Lindsay Evans

Harlequin Kimani Romance

Pleasure Under the Sun
Sultry Pleasure

LINDSAY EVANS

is a traveler, lover of food and avid café loafer. She's been reading romances since she was a very young girl and feels touched by a certain amount of surreal magic in that she now gets to write her own love stories. *Pleasure Under the Sun* was her debut book with Harlequin Kimani Romance.

SULTRY PLEASURE

LINDSAY EVANS

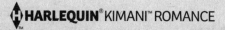
HARLEQUIN® KIMANI™ ROMANCE

For Dorothy Lindsay and Cherie Evans Lyon.
Your encouragement and love lifts me up, always.

Recycling programs
for this product may
not exist in your area.

ISBN-13: 978-0-373-86367-9

SULTRY PLEASURE

Copyright © 2014 by Lindsay Evans

For questions and comments about the quality of this book please contact us
at CustomerService@Harlequin.com.

Printed in U.S.A.

www.Harlequin.com

Dear Reader,

With one selfish and unforgivable act, Diana's father stole her childhood, leaving her broken, yet stronger than ever before. After his betrayal, she built a life for herself from the ground up without anyone's help.

When an irresistible millionaire with laughing eyes and unexpected connections to her previous tragedy walks into her life, Diana must fight to separate her past pain from the very present possibilities of pleasure and love.

The sexy millionaire is a master of seduction. But she has always been the mistress of saying "no." Join me, dear reader, to find out who will win this sensual battle of wills.

Lindsay Evans

Many thanks to Kimberly Kaye Terry for her invaluable help on this journey of mine. Also to Khaulah Naima Nuruddin, Sheree L. Greer, Angela Gabriel, Brook Blander and Keturah Israel—my friends and supporters.
The butterflies in my garden.

Chapter 1

Marcus Stanfield walked into the party already looking for the exits. On a Saturday night in Miami, he'd much rather be on his boat or partying with friends than bleeding away the night at a charity ball he had no real interest in attending. The music was calm and laid-back, acceptable jazz that blended into the background while Miami business professionals and philanthropists wove through the crowd in their formal-dinner wear—black tie and tails, cocktail dresses, diamonds dripping from necks and wrists.

He shifted his shoulders under his unbuttoned black blazer and reached out to take a glass of what he hoped was scotch from one of the passing waiters. He sipped the drink and winced. It *was* scotch but too cheap for his taste. Maybe he wouldn't even last until the awards were announced.

Marcus left the drink on a nearby table and looked around the room, hoping to find Reynaldo March, one of the men being honored at the night's charity banquet and a

VP at his company, Sucram Holdings. As Marcus glanced over the crowd in search of the gray-haired VP, he heard the sound of a woman's laughter, husky and low, nearby.

The woman's laugh was rich and deep, with a hint of naughtiness. A combination that drew him like a bee to honey. His ears latched on to the sound while his eyes tracked the room for its source. Soon he found it.

Two women stood together. One was still laughing, her head thrown back, a hand propped up on her hip. She was slender and pretty, light-skinned with wavy black hair down to the middle of her back. She had a firm and high rear. And she looked money-hungry, like the type who would lie down for a man just because of what was in his wallet. Definitely his usual style.

But, inexplicably, it was the woman standing next to her that drew and kept Marcus's attention. She had dark skin, angelic features and straightened hair pulled back in an elegant French roll. Even from across the room, he sensed her innocence. While her friend was dressed in a purple satin dress that caught her at midthigh and clung to her slender but generously proportioned body, this woman wore ice-blue.

The pale dress drew Marcus's eyes to her deep mahogany skin. The dress was modestly cut just beneath her collar bones, the waist cinched and hem flaring out in frothy blue around her knees. She was tapping her feet to the music.

While her friend laughed with her whole body, this woman only smiled faintly, her full mouth tilting up at the corners with mild amusement. Marcus looked back at the friend with her killer body, white teeth and long hair that fell in thick waves over her luscious breasts. She was definitely more his type, a woman who would want him for his money and never anything else. The safe type.

But he wanted the woman in blue. He fastened his blazer's single button and walked over to them.

"Good evening, ladies," Marcus said, his charming smile firmly in place.

The laughing woman gave him a considering glance, a quick but thorough evaluation of what he was wearing, how he looked, what he was worth. He had been the focus of that look so many times in Miami that he expected it more often than not when meeting someone new.

"Good evening." The woman in purple greeted him, a smile curving her full lips. "You're Marcus, aren't you?"

"I am," he said. "A pleasure to meet you."

The woman he wanted treated him like he was intruding on their conversation. She was even more beguiling up close. Not traditionally beautiful but exquisitely made with her large eyes, wide mouth and narrow chin. Her neck was a long and slender stalk he could easily span with one hand. The top of her head only came as high as his jaw, even in her stilettos.

"I'm Trish," the long-haired one said, offering her hand to shake. "And this is my best friend, Diana." She nudged her friend, as if encouraging her to be nice to Marcus.

Diana looked at her in irritation, then extended her own hand in greeting. "Marcus." Her voice was carefully neutral.

"Don't say my name like that," he said with a grin. "So formal. Especially when I came over here intending to ask you to dance with me."

A frown settled on her angelic face. "I don't dance."

"She'd love to." Trish smiled even wider to make up for Diana's lack of welcome, then nudged her friend again, this time directly into Marcus's arms. "Enjoy, honey!" She grabbed Diana's purse and stood back, looking pleased with herself.

Marcus took Diana's arm and led her to the dance floor, where they were playing Marvin Gaye's "Got to Give It Up." He drew her into his arms, keeping a respectable distance between them but still allowing himself the pleasure of smelling the light rosemary-scented perfume that clung to her skin. Another scent, something sweeter, lingered beneath the hint of fresh herb.

"Thank you for dancing with me," he said.

She looked up at him, her eyes large and serious behind a veil of thick lashes. Her narrow chin jutted out.

"You know very well I didn't agree to dance with you," she said.

"You don't strike me as a woman who'd let herself be talked into something she didn't want to do," he murmured as they moved to the beat of the song. "Whatever small part of you wanted to come with me, I'm grateful for it." He smiled, strangely charmed by her coolness. Her reaction to him was completely different from what he usually got from women.

At his look, Diana pursed her lips, the lines of her face softening. "I'm sorry. It's just been a long day. Everyone here seems to think just because I work for a nonprofit, that means I'm going to whore myself out to the one with the biggest bank account."

Damn. She was definitely *not* his type at all. With other women, he knew what they wanted, and they knew what he could give. Sex for money: a transparent transaction. But he didn't want to let Diana go yet.

"If it makes you feel any better, you don't have to whore yourself out to me at all." Marcus dipped his hips close to hers as they moved to the music, then pulled back. "All I want is a dance."

She looked at him with a hint of doubt in her sparkling brown eyes. "A dance is all you *really* want?"

Marcus smiled. "For now." He spun her around to the rhythm of the song, then pulled her back seamlessly into his arms. "Later I was thinking of trying to tempt you with dinner, maybe a late-night walk on the beach."

The corner of her mouth twitched. "I've already eaten, and I try to avoid the beach at night."

"Why is that?"

She looked at him with a pointed rise of an eyebrow. "Sharks."

Marcus only shook his head, carefully keeping his amusement from showing. "Well, that's where you have me all wrong," he said. "I don't bite. At least not on the first date."

Against her will, Diana Hobbes was getting swept away. Marcus was a charmer. He danced beautifully, a graceful companion as they moved through the steps of the old-school dance, not grandstanding, simply complementing the moves she made, the subtle rocking of her hips and dip of her shoulders. He danced with her like he wanted something and was willing to be patient until he got it.

He was a handsome man. She had noticed that immediately when he came up to her and Trish. Tall and wickedly sexy with eyes the color of old gold rimmed in black. He was obviously one of the rich ones despite his lack of the usual trappings. His blazer and jeans looked like they had been tailored to fit his gym-hard body, and his haircut was crisp and fresh, his nails buff-shined and recently manicured. The jeans and sneakers he wore said he obviously didn't care what people thought, yet no one looked twice at him. She just couldn't tell if he was one of the idle rich or someone who actually worked for his money.

Trish had known immediately who he was, but Diana had no clue. She reminded herself to ask her best friend later exactly who this guy was. In the meantime, the feel of his strong arms around her was intoxicating. The subtle scent of his sandalwood cologne, along with his deep and rumbling voice that pulled answers from her rather than talking about himself, worked magic on her attention-starved body. It had been a long time since a man had paid her such focused attention, especially with Trish around. But she knew it wouldn't last. It never did.

"What about the second date?" she asked. "What should I expect then?"

The question fell from Diana's lips against her will. She bit the inside of her cheek, but it was impossible to take back the words. She didn't want to seem overly interested. Or desperate.

"On the second date, anything can happen," he said with an amused light in his mesmerizing black-rimmed pale eyes. "Are you giving me something to look forward to?"

"Don't get ahead of yourself," she said. Though she might as well have been talking to herself. Just because he was the first man in months to show her this much attention shouldn't be a reason to throw all caution to the wind. Like all the others, once he figured out she didn't have much space in her life for anyone else, he would disappear.

"I never do that," he said. "But I do go after what I want." He looked at her meaningfully. "Can we at least have a first date before we discuss the terms of the second?"

Her fingers tightened briefly on his shoulder through the soft blazer. She had been working harder than usual lately. Giving all her days and even some of her nights to Building Bridges. Never leaving time to find a man, much less cultivating something meaningful and lasting—or just hot and delicious—with one. And then there was her family.

As she opened her mouth to respond to Marcus, the song ended. He took her hand, looked around the room as if searching for someone, then tugged her toward the back of the enormous ballroom and outside to the balcony.

The night was beautiful. A symphony of stars shone in the sky, and the gorgeous Miami skyline lit up like a Christmas tree in December. The balmy breeze brushed over Diana's face and throat.

"Come to dinner with me." The laughter was gone from his voice.

"I'm a little busy right now," she said, though her heart pounded in her chest at his nearness and the urgent way he spoke. She allowed him to pull her close and then closer, overwhelming her with the spicy scent of his aftershave and the heat of his body.

"You are a very compelling woman," he said in his rumbling voice.

"And what is it, Marcus, that makes me so compelling in your eyes?" She meant to tease him, to force him into a tongue-tied mess so he could retreat and put them back on more appropriate footing.

His mouth tucked up at the corners. "Because you insist on saying my name in such a stern way, for one." He moved a hand down her back, eliciting a round of intrigued tremors. "When you say my name, it sounds like I'm in trouble."

"Hmm. Is this better?" She tested the gentler sound of his name on her tongue. Once. Twice.

"Say my name one more time like that and I might have to accelerate this to being our second date. My teeth are aching for a taste."

She shuddered and drew back, her hands falling off his chest and to her sides. She put a few more feet of space between them. His teasing was getting to be more than she

could handle. Yes, she liked him, but she was never one
to rush into something with any man.

"I think you'll have to go hungry this time around,"
she said.

He looked at her with disappointment, sliding his hands
into his pants pockets. He leaned back against the railing
separating them from the brilliant Miami night. "You're
breaking my heart," he said softly. "I hope this isn't something you're going to do all the time."

She turned away from him and toward the rooftop pool,
glittering impossibly blue under the lights. "I don't play
games," she said.

"But games are part of what make life fun." Amusement and temptation laced his voice.

Diana knew she had to get away from this man. She had
danced with him for longer than she planned, had stepped
out to the balcony with him although she'd known it wasn't
a good idea. And it would soon be time for the awards to
be announced. Her boss, the executive director of Building Bridges, wanted to have Diana by her side when the
crystal plaques were presented. She looked past Marcus's
shoulder to see the room resolving itself into order, people
stepping away from the dance floor en masse and heading
into the ballroom, where the round tables and chairs sat.

"I have to go," she said.

He gently grabbed her hand. "Come out with me after
this. I'd like to show you my Miami."

Just then, a gray-haired man with a red rose in his lapel
opened the door behind them and announced that it was
almost time for the awards presentation. Diana felt he had
looked specifically at her and Marcus, although there were
nearly a dozen other people out on the balcony enjoying
the balmy evening.

"We'll see," she said, tugging her hand away.

Diana felt his disappointment but refused to turn around. She slipped inside and made her way quickly into the ballroom and over to the table where her boss was waiting.

"Diana! I've been looking all over the place for you." Nora Evers, elegant and poised in her pearls and iron-gray Chanel dress, held out her hands to grip Diana's. "Come. It's about to start."

Nora's lush figure was downplayed in the severely cut dress, but it was still apparent why the newspapers often called her one of the sexiest women in nonprofit. Her frosted gray hair was cut in a sleek natural style that showed off her long-lashed bedroom eyes and pillowy lips. Her still-youthful body and the way she spoke with someone as if they were the only person in the room made her irresistible to many.

Despite her boss's call for her attention, Diana couldn't resist a last look over her shoulder toward Marcus. Then she deliberately pushed him from her mind and concentrated on the event at hand.

The Prism Award Ceremony and Gala was one of the best attended and most prestigious charity events in Miami. The award honored business people and philanthropists in south Florida for the outstanding charity work they had done for the local community. Although Building Bridges had been doing its work for more than eight years with Nora at the helm for three of those years, this was the first time the organization had been invited to the Prism gala.

It was a well-known fact that when an organization's head was personally invited to the Prism gala, it meant the organization was either being awarded or considered for an award the following year. Either way, Nora and the Building Bridges family were ecstatic. It meant more notice to their small nonprofit, which hopefully would translate into more donations, more interest and more work being done for the children they helped place in loving and safe homes.

As assistant executive director, in addition to her regular duties, Diana had to also be her single boss's "work wife." That included supporting Nora at events like this. She brushed a bit of lint from Nora's shoulder, then sat down at the table they shared with Trish and two other members of the Building Bridges staff.

The round table was set up with a beautiful floral centerpiece, full water glasses in front of each of the five chairs and the proper utensils for the meal to come. They were seated near the middle of the room, not so far to the front as the Gates Foundation but definitely not by the kitchen, either. Diana knew Nora would care about that. She nervously touched the back of her ear, then forced her hand to her lap.

"How was the dance?" Trish appeared at Diana's side. She sat down at the table, sliding both their purses near the table's centerpiece. Her amused whisper was for Diana's ears only.

She bit the inside of her lips to prevent a smile. Her friend was always trying to save her love life, usually with mixed results. "It went well," she said. "He's a good dancer."

"Who's a good dancer?" Nora looked up from her prepared speech, tapping the index cards briefly against the table.

"A man Diana just met." Trish grinned wickedly. "He took her off to the dance floor earlier. I thought he was coming my way, but when he latched on to our sweet girl, I was tickled." The look on her face suggested she wanted to say much more, but she contented herself with making kissing faces when Nora wasn't looking. Diana rolled her eyes, hiding a smile.

"What's his name?" Nora asked.

When Trish told her, Nora's brow furrowed.

"That name sounds familiar." Nora adjusted her pearls at her throat, eyes looking into the middle distance as she thought about who Marcus was. "Ah, yes. That most enterprising young man who owns the boat my friends and I always see sailing the bay early Sunday mornings. The *Dirty Diana,* I think it's called."

Trish chuckled. "Sounds like a match made in heaven." She winked at Diana.

Diana kicked her friend under the table, then deliberately turned to Nora. "He seems interesting," she said.

Nora laughed. "Of course, dear. Even I can see what a lovely piece of man candy that is."

Trish guffawed. "Man candy, for sure. Something for you to suck on, Di?"

Nora cleared her throat, subtly letting Trish know she had gone a little too far. Trish only grinned, unrepentant.

As the women talked, the room quickly filled with some of the wealthiest and most influential citizens of Miami. Their voices rose and fell in conversation and in laughter as they found their seats. Then the clink of water and wineglasses. The faint strains of Tchaikovsky leaked from the speakers overhead while the host from the Prism Foundation, Sheila Beck, stood at the podium, checked the microphone, then gestured to someone Diana couldn't see. Before long, everyone was seated at their respective tables, the conversation and music lulling. Unable to help herself, Diana stretched her neck, looking for Marcus. But she didn't see him.

Marcus stood at the entrance to the ballroom, watching the crowd settle into their seats. From across the room, he saw Diana at the table with her friend, Trish, and three other women. He shook the hands of several men and women he'd done business with over the years and congratulated them on the good work they had been doing.

Although he was supposed to be at the table with Reynaldo and representing his company and his father at the award ceremony, an event where a bunch of rich men and women congratulated each other on the amount of money they were able to write off by tossing peanuts to one cause or another, Marcus was exactly where he wanted to be: watching Diana.

Why did he find her so damn interesting? Marcus asked himself the question as he took in the slender shape of her inclined in a listening pose toward the older woman seated at her table. It could have been that air of innocence about her. The way it made him want to pull her into a dark corner and find out if her lips were as soft as they looked.

"Marcus!"

Reynaldo's voice pulled him from his reverie. The slender, dark-haired man appeared at Marcus's side in his tuxedo, black bow tie against his gleaming white shirt. "I wasn't sure you'd make it."

Marcus hadn't been sure he'd make it either. After a long night and morning at a party in Coconut Grove, he hadn't been in the mood for anything more than his bed. But responsibility had kicked in. He shrugged off his exhaustion, showered and looked over his secretary's notes about what was supposed to happen at the event. The Prism Gala was a good PR opportunity for Sacrum Holdings. His donations to their various charities made his company look good and made *him* look good.

"The committee appreciates your presence," Reynaldo said. "And I do as well."

"Of course." Marcus nodded and shook the man's hand. "Where are we sitting?"

The VP showed him to a table near the front of the room, a brief walk through the large ballroom that felt like a parade. How many CEOs had shown up to see one of their executives honored? Marcus knew he was one of the few and was being looked at positively as a result. The members of the Prism committee may be a tight-assed lot, but they were also very powerful. *You never know when you might need a favor,* Marcus thought as he unbuttoned his blazer and sank into the plush chair at Reynaldo's side.

The ceremony began shortly after they sat, with the music winding all the way down and the conversations tapering off as the host, an excited-looking woman in her mid-forties, Sheila Beck, made her way to the stage and took the microphone. Marcus relaxed in his seat, bracing his elbows on top of the table as he looked around the crowded ballroom.

It was a sea of sameness. Tuxedos, gray dresses and black dresses, pearls, jewels, the occasional flare of a pale blue or green dress, the women for the most part keeping to the traditional muted tones, even though this was Miami. Marcus had no respect for such boring presentation.

Instead of traditional black tie, he wore what he wanted. A red handkerchief in the pocket of his black blazer, the white button-down shirt open at the collar. Black jeans and high-top Jordans. Needlessly rebellious, he knew, but it made him feel better about being trapped indoors for something like this when he'd rather be out making money or playing on his boat.

His eyes found Diana a few tables back. She was watching him. He grinned but she quickly looked away, fiddling with her earring. When he failed to compel her to look at him again through the power of his stare alone, he turned his attention back to the ceremony.

Sheila Beck and her fellow committee members put on a good show. Lively and fast. Reynaldo received his award to much applause while Sacrum Holdings was unexpectedly honored as one of the most environmentally sound companies in Miami. Instead of leaving like he'd originally planned, Marcus sat in his seat, held prisoner by the slim possibility that Diana would go somewhere with him after the ceremony.

Applause. Speeches. The apparent surprise award to one of the women sitting at Diana's table—a gray-haired woman with more style than half the women in the room, although she did wear the least offensive color imaginable. Marcus took note of the organization, the woman's name and the fact that she took her time as she grasped the crystal statuette in hands that shook. The woman was gracious on the stage, and brief. She thanked each of her staff by name, including Diana Hobbes, who was apparently the assistant executive director of Building Bridges. Interesting.

Building Bridges was one of the nonprofits he donated to every year. Small world.

As soon as the ceremony was over, Marcus made his way over to Diana's table. Most of the gala's attendees still lingered in the ballroom, grabbing one last drink from the open bar or rabidly shaking as many well-connected hands as they could.

Diana was still seated and talking quietly with her boss. As Marcus moved toward her, he was struck again by how delicate and delicious she looked. His imagination easily conjured what it would be like to walk up to her and kiss the back of her neck, inhale the evocative scent of her perfume, peel that ice-blue dress from her body. He stopped

just behind her chair and greeted the other women around
the table with a nod and smile.

"How about that midnight walk on the beach?" he
asked, resting his hands on the back of her chair.

Diana drew in a breath of surprise but did not bother
to look at him. She glanced instead at her boss and then
at her friend Trish, who smirked up at Marcus.

"I can't," Diana said. "I have to wrap things up here
with Nora," she said.

Her boss waved a dismissive hand. "No, you don't. Take
a little time to yourself this evening. It's been a long and
hard road to get here. Enjoy yourself." She gave a naughty
grin of her own.

"Yes, *please* do," Trish said, staring pointedly at her
friend.

"Well, Diana, it looks like the only resistance is you,"
he said, finally able to meet her eyes, which were a deep,
velvet brown. "I would really enjoy your company tonight."

"Go ahead, Di," Trish said. "A night with this one won't
bring an end to your carefully constructed world, I promise."

Diana flinched as if her friend had touched a nerve. She
bit her lip. "Okay," she said. "But I don't do the beach."
She allowed him to grasp her hand and help her to her feet.

Marcus smiled at Diana's boss and at her friend. "Thank
you for the encouragement, ladies. Have a wonderful
night."

"You, too," Trish said with a wink.

Diana made a strangled noise. "I'll see you on Monday,
Nora. I'll be in early to make sure the photos from tonight
are up on the website and the copy is ready for the news-
letter and press release."

Her boss waved her off. "Of course you will."

Trish stood up and slapped Diana on the butt. "I'll expect you to give me *all* the details tonight."

Marcus laughed. "You ready?"

"Yes," Diana said, giving her friend the side eye.

He offered her his arm and, after a moment's hesitation, she took it. With her purse clutched in her hand, she walked out of the ballroom with him.

Plums, he realized after a few moments walking at her side through the thinning crowd. She smelled like rosemary and plums. A delicious and fresh sweetness that he had the sudden urge to sink his teeth into. Marcus licked his lips.

"So," he said to distract himself from her scent and the imagined flavor she would leave behind on his tongue. "Why don't you *do* the beach? You can't swim?"

"I can swim," she said. "I just choose not to."

"Why?"

"I think it's too early yet for that kind of conversation, don't you?" She looked at him sideways.

"Not at all," Marcus said. "The sooner I know what you don't like and why, the better I can plan our next date. So now I know not to plan a romantic dinner for you on my boat."

"Oh, God, no!"

A man and a young woman who looked like his mistress were already waiting for the elevator when they got there. The woman was beautifully put together in her tight white dress and red heels, her shoulder-length brown hair the same shade as her skin. But there was something almost desperate in the way she clung to him. Marcus nodded in greeting to both while Diana exchanged smiles with them.

"What about an afternoon on the sand?" Marcus asked, continuing their conversation. "No water, just a picnic and a bottle of wine."

"No."

He tipped his head to look down at her in curiosity. "Really?"

When the elevator arrived, Marcus held the door open and waited for both women to get into the car ahead of him. After the other man got in behind him, he pressed the button for the lobby. Classical music played as the car descended toward the main floor. The elevator's mirrored surfaces reflected the two couples studiously avoiding each other's eyes.

"So what do you like?" Marcus asked.

"Simple things," Diana said after a brief glance at the other occupants of the elevator.

Marcus took the opportunity of the silent ride to properly look his fill of Diana Hobbes. The skin like silk. Her large eyes, high cheekbones and sensuous mouth in the face that was straight from his boyhood dreams. Angelic. Kind. But Diana seemed serious. More serious than anyone he ever thought he'd be interested in. But there was something about her wide mouth, about the way she seemed to want him but didn't *want* to want him.

The elevator bell announced their floor just before the doors slid open. Marcus guided her toward the front of the hotel and the valet. He gave the blue-jacketed boy his valet ticket and stood aside to wait with Diana while his car was brought around.

It was another warm Miami night. Already, Marcus felt like shrugging off the blazer, rolling up the sleeves of his shirt and getting comfortable. In her pale blue dress, Diana already looked comfortable in the heat, even relieved to be out in it.

Inside the hotel, she had been cold. It had been impossible for him not to notice her tight nipples under the thin dress. The hard points had drawn his eyes more than once.

And he had hoped she wouldn't think him rude or a complete pervert for staring at her breasts when he should have been meeting her eyes. His initial impulse had been to give her his blazer, but the primitively male part of him didn't want to deny himself the sight of her, an ice queen in her glacier-blue dress, with her vulnerable nipples pressing against the cloth.

"So why no water?" he finally asked after they waited in silence for a moment.

"I'll tell you when we know each other better," she said with a faint smile.

"Fair enough," he said. "I look forward to that deepening relationship."

She looked up at him, meeting his eyes with her cool brown gaze. Something moved in his chest, but he forced himself not to look away.

"Here you are, sir." The valet appeared beside them, eager and smiling.

"Thank you." Marcus slipped him a twenty-dollar bill.

He guided Diana toward the passenger side of the silver Mercedes SLR, which already had both doors open. She climbed in with barely a glance at the car, and he shut her door before getting behind the wheel.

"Thank you for coming out with me tonight," he said. "You won't regret it."

She looked at him, the corners of her eyes crinkling faintly. "Is that a promise?"

"Absolutely." The car started with a delicate purr and slid away from the curb.

Chapter 2

It was late. After the light dinner she'd barely touched at the award ceremony, and after not eating anything prior to the ceremony because she'd been too busy preparing for it, Diana was starving. She snuck a peek at her watch and saw it was already past eleven. Much later than when she would normally eat, but that didn't make her hunger any less urgent.

In the seat next to her, Marcus looked like the kind of man who lived most of his life after dark. He seemed all energy and sophistication. One of those men she'd heard about who populated Miami like sand on the beach. But despite living in Miami all her life, this was her first chance to meet one of his breed.

"Are we going out for food?" she asked with a touch of eagerness.

"Yes," he said, briefly moving his eyes from the road to flash her a smile. "A simple place."

She raised an eyebrow, remembering the words she had

said to him while at the hotel. Yes, she liked simple things. But she sensed a man like Marcus did not. His money afforded him the world—what could he know about the plain ways to make a woman like her happy?

She was counting on that to kill her attraction to him even though, as she sat in his car rich with the smell of new leather, her skin felt nearly electric at his presence. She watched him without him being aware of it, noting again his luscious deep-brown complexion, sculpted mouth, golden eyes that were narrow and short-lashed beneath his prominent brow. His hair was neatly cut, an attractive and undoubtedly expensive style, and his clothes screamed money.

And he was going to take her somewhere simple? Diana's mouth twitched as she wondered if he even knew what simple was.

Marcus skillfully navigated the car through the streets of downtown Miami, across the bridge that afforded an incredible view of the water lit with lights. Diana sighed. Although she hated the water, the view of Miami at night never ceased to awe her. It was one of the most beautiful cities she'd ever seen, packed with gorgeous people, good food and wine and incredible experiences just waiting to be sampled.

The car pulled up in front of a restaurant that had a line of people waiting to get in that extended halfway down the block. A valet approached the car, opening Marcus's door and then Diana's. They got out and he gave the slim woman in a fitted tuxedo outfit the keys to the Mercedes.

Marcus slid the valet ticket into his pants pocket. Then, almost as an afterthought, he shrugged off his blazer and threw it in the backseat of the car. He thanked the valet, then walked with Diana to the back of the long line.

* * *

As Marcus joined her in line, Diana looked at him in surprise and admiration. She'd expected him to approach the front of the line and demand to be seated immediately. Her estimation of him rose.

"What is this place?" she asked

"This is Gillespie's," he said. "A nice and *simple* lounge where we can have a bite to eat, get to know each other and spend the evening together without being on the water."

She didn't rise to the teasing bait in his voice. "Sounds nice," she murmured, amused despite herself.

"I hope you'll think so when we get in."

As they waited in line, Diana noticed that a few newcomers left their expensive cars and headed directly to the door, expecting star treatment. But they didn't get it. People already waiting gave each other knowing looks as the newcomers were directed to the back of the line.

A couple of D-list movie stars were up ahead of her and Marcus. A musician whose song was on rotation on Top 40 stations. And many women who looked like models, tall and haughty with beautifully applied makeup and rich-looking men on their arms.

The line moved quickly, and it wasn't long before they were inside. Gillespie's turned out to be more than a restaurant; it was also a lounge and jazz bar. A moody piano played over the speakers, audible through the voices riding the air, setting a sophisticated and mellow mood. Diana liked it right away. The hostess, a gorgeous brown-skinned woman with her long hair twisted in a bun, showed them to a table upstairs that overlooked the stage.

The delicious smell of food wove through the restaurant. As Diana opened her menu, a waiter walked past with a cast-iron skillet sizzling with a mixture of green peppers, onions and shrimp. Diana's stomach growled. She blushed and looked up at Marcus. He was watching her.

"You're not looking at the menu," she said.

"I already know what I want." His steady look made it clear exactly what he was talking about.

The heat in her face burned even hotter, but she kept her voice level. "The only thing you'll have in your mouth tonight is listed right there." She dipped her head toward the closed menu in front of him.

"That sounds very discouraging," he said with a low laugh.

"I'm just letting you know not to expect anything more than dinner tonight."

He shrugged. "The pleasure of your company is all I need."

She rolled her eyes and lifted the menu to look at the offerings. It wasn't long before their waitress appeared. Marcus placed his order still without looking at the menu. After a hesitating moment, Diana ordered something that looked decent but wasn't too expensive.

She didn't want him thinking that just because he paid for a fifty-dollar steak, he was entitled to lay her on her back at the end of the night. Although she worked in the nonprofit world and often relied on rich men and women to keep the good work of the foundation going, she knew all too well that most of them would commodify any woman if given the chance. If they wanted her, those rich people assumed she had a price. Granted, she'd never felt the delicate thrums of attraction for one of them before.

"Why don't you trust me?" he asked.

"Who said I don't trust you?" She looked at him with studied innocence.

He chuckled, tilting his head to look at her with his brilliant eyes. "I like you, Diana. I enjoy your company. If at any point you don't like what's going on tonight, you can just get up and go. I'll call you a taxi and that will be that."

His kindness suddenly made her feel ridiculous. She took a sip of the champagne he'd ordered for them and looked around the restaurant. On stage, a woman had joined the pianist, singing a soulful version of Nina Simone's "My Baby Just Cares for Me."

Looking down at the performance, she realized that most of the crowd was actually paying attention to the music, pausing their conversations and their meals to watch the woman with a head of blazing red hair vamp it up while her husky and sensual voice made an invitation out of the song.

"I like it here," she said after a few minutes watching the singer. "Thank you for bringing me."

"You're welcome."

After their meal came, they sat in a comfortable quiet, allowing the music to fill the spaces between them. The food—a creamy onion soup rich with the taste of butter and garlic, and seared scallops simmered in orange butter and served on a bed of edamame and quinoa—was delicious, probably one of the best meals she'd ever eaten.

Marcus offered to share his braised lamb shank served with red cabbage and gorgeous golden polenta. She declined but watched him eat his meal with obvious pleasure, slowly savoring each bite and licking his lips before taking a sip of the wine.

After the waitress took their dinner plates away, they sat back with drinks to enjoy the performances on the stage. Diana sipped her champagne, sweetly relaxed in her chair as she turned her head to listen to the delicate, intertwined voices of the twin girls, no older than teenagers, who were singing now. She felt Marcus's eyes on her, a gentle weight, but she did not look up.

"Dance with me," he said.

In that moment, she couldn't imagine saying no to him. He guided her to the dance floor near the main stage, where there were only a dozen or so people already dancing. Marcus opened his arms, and she stepped into them.

The twins sang a slow and lulling version of "Blue Gardenia," one of them sitting on the edge of the stage with her cordless microphone while the other swayed on her feet in front of the corded mic, her voice wrapping the room in a velvet curtain of sound. Their voices were low and deep, surprising for such small girls. Diana tried to focus on them instead of the man whose arms were wrapped around her.

Unlike the last time they danced, she felt an intimacy between them, their bodies moving in slow communion to the strains of the jazz song. He smelled solid and warm, spicy, like cedar and sandalwood.

She pulled his scent into her, unable to help herself. He didn't pull her into him and force his crotch into hers, only held her delicately, allowing their bodies to come close during the song, then drift back apart. They swayed, and she smelled him. They turned, and his warmth flowed over her. His hand pressed into the small of her back while his thighs brushed against hers during the dance. A whisper of his breath moved at her ear.

"You are beautiful," he murmured.

And God help her, she believed him.

She slipped her arms around his neck and moved closer, a little horrified that she was so susceptible to flattery. But it felt good that this handsome man thought she was beautiful and wanted to spend time with her. She was enjoying his company. When the song ended, they kept dancing by silent agreement, moving even more slowly as the singers took on a Sade song, "Lover's Rock."

Their hips swayed together. Flutters of arousal moved through Diana's belly, made her skin tingle whenever it touched his. She knew she should be worried, that she should move away from him and regain control of herself, but it felt too good. His touch. The music. The desire winding around them like a silken ribbon.

The song ended and Marcus slid his hands around her waist, pressed his mouth to her forehead.

"I want to kiss you," he murmured.

She trembled at the urgency in his voice. Her hands tightened for a moment on his shoulders. Her body was hot with the need for that kiss. "Not here," she said, not sure how she would react to his touch in front of all those people.

He pulled back, took her hand and drew her through the thin crowd of dancers. Down a quiet, wood-paneled hallway. The smell of cigars and wood smoke. Emptiness. He pressed her against the wall, hips against hers, hands planted on either side of her head. His mouth swooped down, lightly touching hers and sweetly asking permission.

Diana parted her lips with a sigh. A sound of pure masculine pleasure rumbled through him as they kissed. Mouths fiercely joined, tongues twining together. He touched her hips, hands hard and warm on her. Arousal rippled through her. She sank her nails into his back through the thin shirt and he made another rough sound, then shoved his hips into hers.

What are you doing?

A part of her rebelled against what she was falling into. But the rest of her rejoiced. She squeezed her thighs together as the arousal built. He licked her mouth, sucking on her tongue, sending a molten feeling straight into her lap. She wanted his hands on her. She wanted him inside her. But…but that couldn't happen. She wasn't that kind of girl.

Diana forced herself to pull away from him, palms pressed to his chest, easing away to dim the fires of the sudden and consuming desire.

"Christ! You're so damn sexy...." He breathed the words against her mouth.

"You're not so bad yourself." She bit the inside of her lip to stop herself from inviting him home with her. It had been so long since she'd been with a man she was attracted to like this, a man who was attracted to her in return. Diana dug her fingers into his biceps.

"I want to spend the night with you," he rasped.

She shook her head, but before the words could pass her lips, he squeezed her waist. "Not like *that.* Well, I'd like that, but I would settle for seeing the sunrise with you." He said it as if surprised by the desire. By her. "I want to make the night last."

"Yes," she said softly. "Yes. I want that, too."

He looked relieved. "Good."

As they walked back to the table, her phone vibrated through her purse. She thought about ignoring it, but the years of being the responsible one in her family wore her down. She took out the phone.

It was a text from her brother, Jason. She already had a missed call from him. His car had broken down somewhere in Coconut Grove, and he wanted her to come get him.

Diana's jaw tightened as she read her brother's message. There was no way she could ignore it. But with the fires of possibility burning between her and Marcus, she was tempted to. She bit back a groan of disappointment.

"I have to go," she said as they got to their table.

Marcus looked at her in surprise, and she winced. Why tonight, of all nights, did Jason need her? If she didn't know any better, she'd think her brother knew she was *this* close to finally getting some and wanted to screw things up for her.

Marcus put money on the table for their bill. "I'll take you back to your car." She saw disappointment on his face, a naked and vulnerable look, but he didn't say anything else.

"It's my brother," she said softly, feeling the need to explain about her sudden exit. Diana shrugged. "I have to go to him."

"Family is important," Marcus said. He pulled her into him, kissed her lightly on the mouth, then pressed briefly into her as if he wanted and needed more. "You don't have to explain."

She was glad for his understanding, but she wanted to scream. Her brother knew he could count on her for so much that he often turned to her instead of taking care of the simplest things himself. Like this. Why hadn't he called AAA and used the membership she had gotten him a couple of years ago when he'd first gone off to college? She sighed quietly and wrapped a hand around Marcus's solid arm, compelled to touch him even if it was in the most innocuous way.

"Thank you," she said.

"No. Thank you for coming out with me tonight. I know you had other plans."

"This is much better than the night I had planned. There definitely was no unlimited champagne at the office."

He smiled. "If you want, I can take care of that for you. I can arrange for a Dom Perignon fountain at your desk so you can think of me every time the bubbles hit your tongue."

His words made her flush with reaction. They made her recall the recent taste of him on her tongue. The twisting shaft of heat that had flared into her as his tongue stroked her mouth. She lifted a hand to toy with her earring, a distraction from reaching out to touch him, to pull him back to that dark corner of the restaurant for more kisses. More everything.

"That's a little too decadent for me," she said when she could finally speak again.

"I'm sure you'd get used to it fast." He was talking about something else, seducing her, and she was allowing it to happen.

Diana grabbed her purse more tightly, cleared her throat. If she stayed in his presence any longer, she just might let her brother fend for himself. "Are you ready?"

At her car in the hotel parking garage, Diana fought the feeling of regret. She didn't want to leave Marcus. But instead of dwelling on what could not happen, she got on her tiptoes to share a good-night kiss with him. A sweet, lingering kiss.

"I want to see you again," he said, his arms wrapped tightly around her.

A warmth grew in her belly at his tone. It was a heady feeling, knowing that he wanted her. No other man had ever been that passionate about being in her company; none had shown such urgency and desire for her. It was flattering. And sexy beyond belief.

Diana gave him her number. "Call me," she said.

"I'll call you tomorrow." He slipped his cell phone back into his pocket. "Or maybe later on tonight."

Diana kissed his mouth again, pulling back before he could deepen their contact, then she opened her car door. "Talk with you soon."

"Count on it." Marcus stepped back, sliding his hands in his pants pockets.

Under the bright lights of the garage, he was even more handsome. Golden-brown skin. The top lip of his full mouth thinner than the lower. His face sculpted and regal like the statue of an Egyptian pharaoh she'd once seen on the History channel.

Diana forced her gaze away from him. She climbed into her Nissan SUV before she could change her mind, started her car with trembling hands and drove away.

Chapter 3

Diana rolled over in bed, her short yellow nightgown twisting around her torso, tugging at her breasts. Still mostly asleep, she bit her lip and kept her eyes closed as the sensation of being bound in her clothes meshed with the fantasies playing behind her eyelids. Marcus kissing her. His body pinning hers to the bed while his hand slipped between her thighs.

Her lashes fluttered open, her lips parted, her thighs pressed together as she conjured Marcus. His golden eyes. His kiss. How she had not wanted the previous night to end. As she remembered how he had caressed her sensitive nape during their slow and intense kiss, she squirmed against the sheets.

Another movie flickered behind her eyelids. Marcus sliding his hands under her dress as he pressed her against the wall at Gillespie's. His masculinity hot and hard against her belly, his tongue sweet in her mouth.

The phone rang then, jolting her against the bed. At

first, she ignored it, savoring the remnants of the dream. Then her eyes flew open.

What if it was Marcus calling?

She jumped up and ran toward the urgent ringing from the kitchen counter. But by the time she got to the phone, the ringer stopped. She looked at the screen.

It had been her mother. She didn't even think about calling her back.

With a drag to her step, she walked through her bedroom to the bathroom. There, she used the toilet, washed her hands and stared at her lips in the mirror, imagining they were still swollen from last night's passionate kisses.

Last night. Marcus. Her brother's interruption.

She sighed, abruptly feeling her body's exhaustion.

Diana leaned heavily against the sink. Between her brother's call for help, his rambling conversation afterward and her preoccupation with her date with Marcus, she should be dead to the waking world. But she was wide awake, eagerly anticipating Marcus's call.

Last night, in more ways than one, she had not been pleased. After driving through the congested streets of Coconut Grove, she found her brother with his foot propped against a fire hydrant, the blinkers of his rusty old Buick flashing, the hood up. But he was talking to a woman. Some pretty young thing in a short skirt and with a glint of gold in her mouth.

Diana waited with Jason until the tow truck came, followed the truck to the mechanic's, then drove her brother home to his little one-bedroom apartment in the middle of the Black Grove. And, of course, she hadn't been able to simply drop him off. He wanted her to come in for a drink, to take a seat on his ratty sofa and talk about their mother, about life, even the field trip he and other budding marine biologists at the university had taken earlier that week. By the time Diana had staggered home, it was after five o'clock in the morning.

Barely three hours later, she was, unfortunately, very awake. With her cell phone in hand—she could *almost* convince herself she wasn't waiting for Marcus's call— she walked through her small house, the tiles cool under her bare feet. In the kitchen, she put the ingredients for her morning smoothie in the blender.

She was swallowing a second mouthful when the phone rang. A surge of anticipation darted through her as she grabbed the phone.

But it wasn't Marcus. It was her mother. Again.

"Good morning, Mama." She tried her best not to sound disappointed as she sagged against the counter.

"Diana, what were you thinking?" Cheryl Hobbes-Freeman's angry voice snapped at her through the phone.

"What?"

"I'm looking at you in the paper. How could you?"

"How could I what?" She set her glass on the kitchen counter, confused. What was her mother talking about now? "Slow down and explain yourself, Mama. I have no idea what you're talking about."

Although she didn't know what this latest problem was, Diana could easily picture her mother's ruffled state. Hands wildly gesturing as she walked the circular path of her backyard garden. Surrounded by her tall hibiscus bushes and towering bright red ginger plants, her slender figure already dressed in a T-shirt and cropped pants despite the early hour. The only concession to the morning would be that her always neatly pressed silver hair was still wrapped in a silk scarf from the night before.

"The newspaper!" her mother said shrilly, her voice rising through the phone. She lived all the way in Hialeah, but the way her tone cut, she might as well have been stand-ing in Diana's kitchen. "Don't tell me you haven't seen it."

She heaved a sigh, even after all this time not fully able to deal with her mother's dramatics. Jason got a B in Chemistry—complain to the principal! Her sister, Luna, was five minutes late from school—call the police! Diana looked around her brightly lit kitchen, the pristine cream countertops, the curtains open to let in the brilliant sun-shine. She silently fought against the infection of her moth-er's mania.

"My paper just came, but I haven't read it," she said.

"Get the paper," her mother commanded. "Open it to the society page."

Society page? Her mother only bought the Sunday *Her-ald* for the mountains of coupons she could get her hands on. Remarried to a man who happily supported her, she didn't need to clip coupons. But it gave her something to do with her days aside from gardening and talking on the phone to each of her three children at least once a week. Children she only saw every six months or so by mutual agreement.

Diana opened the paper. As she turned to the page, her mother practically shouted into her ear.

"Do you see it? Do you?"

The paper had photos from the previous night's party. The headline read Prism Luminaries Shine at Annual Miami Philanthropists' Gala.

The headline said just about the same thing every year. The photos and article about the gala took up all the first page of the society section. It had pictures of the wom-en's dresses, their jewelry, a rundown of who was who, which man was single and which couples looked radiant that night. Diana skimmed over the words to the photos. And froze.

Someone had taken a photo of her and Marcus. To be fair, it wasn't just of them, there were four other couples, too, because the paper seemed to be especially focused on speculating about the marriage situation of each pair pictured. The camera had caught her after the party, of course. She was in front of the hotel and in midstep, Marcus's hand on the small of her back as he guided her into his gleaming silver car.

It was a lucky shot. The photographer had caught her looking up at Marcus, a half smile on her lips while his face was seriousness itself, filled with a suave confidence that she'd fought against nearly the entire night. Nothing was scandalous about their pose, although it was obvious they were leaving the gala and heading somewhere together. Under their photo, a suggestive caption showed the newspaper had done its research: *Miami billionaire playboy and business mogul Marcus Stanfield escorts Diana Hobbes, assistant executive director of local non-profit Building Bridges, from the gala and off to a night on the town.*

Diana touched the grainy surface of the paper that memorialized what had happened between her and Marcus last night. She didn't see what was wrong with the photograph. It wasn't as if the papers had speculated that she and Marcus were dashing off from the party to have a wild night of sex.

"Mother—" She made her voice placating.

"You don't know who he is, do you?"

"He's just Marcus, Mama. I met him last night." Diana was getting irritated at her mother's suggestion that she had done something wrong, that she should already know what that thing was and be groveling on her knees because of it.

"Turn the page," her mother snapped.

On the next page, the reporters were done with the

frivolous details of the Prism Gala and now talked about the powerful people there, their money and their business deals. There was another photo of Marcus, this time taken with another man. The two men had been caught side by side, in mid-conversation at what could have been a cocktail party. Marcus had a glass of dark liquor in his hand while the other man was caught in midgesture, his empty hands chopping the air. The other man was older, a couple of inches shorter than Marcus and wore power like his own skin. He was handsome but coldly so—his harder face was all too familiar to Diana. Her eyes dipped lower on the page to read the caption under the photograph: *Power runs in the family. Multibillionaire businessman Quentin Stanfield and his son, Marcus.*

She sagged against the counter. Marcus was Quentin Stanfield's son? Diana made a strangled noise. "But— but…"

"But nothing!" her mother shouted. "That man who had his hands all over you last night is *his* son. That bastard who ruined your father and drove him to shove that gun in his mouth."

Diana shook her head in denial. No, he couldn't be. Their night had been too perfect. *He* had been perfect.

"You can't see him again," her mother said.

Something caught in Diana's throat. "No, I…I won't." She swallowed. "Listen, Mama. I have to go now. I have something I need to do."

Her mother's tone instantly changed. "Are you all right?" She abruptly swung from manic to reasonable in a head-spinning moment, something else Diana had never gotten used to.

"It's not because of what I said, is it?" Her voice was muffled, as if she was pressing her mouth too close to the phone. "If that's what it is, you only met him last night. It should be easy to toss this one back." Her mother paused. "He's a bad seed, baby. Just like Quentin Stanfield. You don't have to end up like your father because of him."

Diana wanted to tell her mother how ridiculous and unlikely it was for her to end up like her father. Suicide at the age of forty-two had left behind three children and a mentally precarious wife. No one could do that to her, but because of what his father had done, she couldn't see Marcus again. She just couldn't.

Her fingers curled into the edge of the kitchen counter. "I'm fine, Mama. I just woke up too soon, that's all. I'm going to get off the phone now. I'll talk with you later, okay?"

"Okay. But call me. Otherwise I'm coming over."

But they both knew how idle that threat was. Her mother had created a stable life with her second husband and rarely left her house.

Diana could only nod as she clutched the phone to her ear. She stared down at the newspaper with the photo of Marcus and his father. The two men looked nothing alike. Nothing. But that didn't prevent the truth from being what it was. Quentin Stanfield had killed her father as surely as if he had put the gun in Washington Hobbes's mouth and pulled the trigger himself.

She slowly put the phone down, seeing in her mind's eye her clinically depressed and suicidal father walk out of their house for the last time. Cheated out of his pension and unable to work, Washington Hobbes had only seen one route to escape his troubles. And it was a route Quentin Stanfield had shown him.

Because of this, Diana couldn't have anything to do with his son.

Chapter 4

Marcus woke late for his own party. By the time he roused himself from his bed, practiced his tai chi and made it outside for the brunch festivities, it was well past two in the afternoon. But his efficient staff had worked their usual miracle, creating a shaded oasis on the grass with tables, tents to shade his fifty plus guests from the sun and more food and drinks than they could reasonably consume while a DJ played smooth R&B from the raised stage. Maxwell, fresh from his recent European tour, stood by the side of the pool, shades over his face, while a few groupies and members of his entourage gathered around him. He was set to perform after brunch.

Biscayne Bay glimmered in the afternoon brightness, its waters splashing with a soft and soothing sound against his tethered yacht and the dock. A small boat floated past the house in the water, its sails a sharp whiteness against the Miami cityscape.

Marcus was chill—mellow and relaxed from his night

with Diana. And although his body had been primed to have sex with her, in the light of morning, he still felt satisfied. Refreshed. Her effect on him was damn near miraculous.

But he knew he should leave her alone. She was nothing like the cotton-candy women who floated in and out of his bed, glad for a taste of the luxurious life before they went on to something else. Diana was serious and passionate, and eventually she would want something from him. Something he couldn't give.

For now, though, he ached to get his hands on her again.

Standing on the pool deck, Marcus stretched under the bright sun, felt the thick muscles in his back flex and release under his shirt and his abs tighten, pecs leaping and settling with his movements. He released a long breath. It was already a good day.

"Are you showing off that sexy manliness just for us?" A vaguely familiar voice broke into his thoughts. He turned from his view of the bay to see a woman he'd once spent a long weekend with. Cassandra something. Or was it Christina?

She was a pretty girl with long, loose black hair, wearing a red bikini top and tiny shorts. She had a friend with her—a blonde with a short, asymmetrical haircut but otherwise similar to his former playmate. Her white bikini showed off well-augmented breasts and a flat stomach decorated with a diamond belly ring.

Marcus knew he once thought Cassandra/Christina was gorgeous, definitely sexy enough to invite into his bed, but compared to Diana's understated elegance, both women looked like they were trying too hard.

"Not this time," he said in response to the question.

"Why, honey? We'd love to see what you've got to

show." She approached him with a bold look on her face, wetting her lips.

Her friend was a little more cautious, but he could see from the way they were looking at him what was on their mind. Not long ago he would have taken them up on their offer, but he wasn't interested. Marcus stepped back and jerked his head toward Maxwell, who was laughing with a couple of guys from the band.

"I'm not feeling that today," Marcus said. "But maybe the star could use some love."

The friend shook her head, bangs fluttering down over one eye. "We already tried. We'd have to get in line." The woman's eyes drifted over Marcus's body, then settled for a long moment at his crotch before meeting his eyes. "The line is shorter over here."

Marcus was instantly repelled. "Sounds like a nice offer," he said sardonically. "But I'm not taking any applications today. It's all about the party and Maxwell."

She bit her lip, still looking him over. "That's too bad."

Cassandra/Christina pressed her luck, too. "Come on, Marcus." She stepped close to him, slid a hand under his shirt and touched his bare stomach. "We can spend some time in the pool house, all three of us. Then maybe go shopping in the morning." The muscles of his belly clenched at her touch, and he just barely stopped himself from shoving her hand away.

"Like I said before, no, thanks." Then he removed her hand from under his shirt and walked away.

By six he was ready for everyone to leave. But, of course, they were just getting started. Women were already swimming naked in the pool while half the party danced on the long patio to the DJ's sounds. All Marcus wanted to do was talk to Diana.

When he finally got a free moment, he took his phone from his pocket, walked away from the sounds of the party and dialed Diana's number. But Marcus got her voice mail. He called her three more times throughout the evening but never reached her.

By the time the party ended at nearly six in the morning, he was half wondering if she'd given him the right number. But it *was* her voice that greeted him each time.

Bleary from alcohol and not enough sleep, he called the private detective he kept on retainer and asked for everything about Diana. Her address, all her phone numbers, where she worked, even her parents' information. Tomorrow, he would find her.

Marcus pulled up to the large, white, two-story Craftsman house that looked newly built, a graceful building that stood out like a swan among the older, weathered ugly-duckling houses on the street. The house's only resemblance to its neighbors was the presence of black "burglar" bars over every one of its wide windows. A sign nearly as tall as the house itself with the words *Building Bridges* stenciled across it in dark blue stood proudly in the front yard.

The neighborhood held the quiet of late morning. It was too early for the kids to be out of school, too early even for the lunch crowd that would walk the streets to the nearby corner store. Not far from the building, a group of boys leaned against a front gate. Their pants sagged and hair was knotted up in dreadlocks, and most of them wore the uniform of backward baseball cap, white undershirt and oversize shorts.

Marcus gave them a nod as he strode toward Building Bridges, pocketing the keys to his car. Three empty rocking chairs waited to be filled on the front porch of the im-

maculate house. The wooden floors of the porch gleamed
with polish, and a bronze mailbox sat just above the doorbell. Marcus rang the bell and waited. A young woman
appeared in the doorway.

She was slender and short with skin the soft brown of
the outside of a coconut. The girl had her hair pulled back
in a ponytail that emphasized her doe eyes and rounded
cheeks. Wearing a white blouse, black skirt and sensible
shoes, she looked like she belonged in a Catholic high
school. Or maybe middle school.

"Good morning." She greeted him with a smile, pushing wide the screen door. Marcus caught the edge of the
door and held it open.

"Good morning." He smiled back at her. "Is Diana
Hobbes working today?"

"Of course!" The girl looked even more pleased, as if
she was glad he had asked for Diana in particular. "She's
always working." She shoved the screen door wider for
him to step through. "Come in."

She introduced herself as Carla as he followed her inside. He gave her his name in return.

Marcus stepped into an open hallway with stairs on the
right leading to the second level of the building. Whereas
the exterior of the building was a crisp white, the interior
was an explosion of color. Each wall was painted a different shade, and the tile floors gleamed black.

The house buzzed with activity and conversation, excited and urgent. A pair of women rushed past him and
up the stairs as they volleyed words. Their heels clacked
against the stairs. From behind the pastel-green wall,
he heard the whispering of printers and fingers tapping
against keyboards. Very faintly, a radio or stereo played
smooth jazz.

"Sorry!" Carla said as she sat behind the reception desk

in the wide hallway. She scooted her chair closer to the
desk. "It's been a little crazy since Prism this weekend.
We didn't expect to win at all, and now we barely know
what to do with ourselves." She grinned.

"I'm sure you'll figure it out." He knew that a Prism
award also came with ten thousand dollars donated toward
the winning foundation's operating costs.

"We're very excited!" Carla clapped her hands. "Are
you here to take Diana out to celebrate?"

"That wasn't the plan, but I'm open to that." He returned the young woman's grin. "The company of a beautiful woman like Diana would make my day even better."

"It would!" The young woman leaned toward him and
filled their shared space with the scent of bubble gum and
hot chocolate. "She is such an amazing person," Carla
said. "Always working long hours, even after everyone
else is gone. She's tireless. If you ask me, I think she's the
person bringing in most of our donations." She said all
these things as if confessing a secret. "And she deserves
a nice lunch."

Just then, he caught a glimpse of Diana upstairs. A flash
of her long legs in pale green high heels, the swish of a
black skirt. A ruffled blouse the same color as her shoes.
Her high heels tapped against the tiled floor as she walked
across the wide space and disappeared into an office. She
looked busy and professional. Like temptation itself. He
wanted to pull her into his arms to kiss her breathless.

"There she is," he said, inclining his head in Diana's
direction.

"Just give me a few minutes while I call her down. I'm
sure she'd love to talk with you."

He abruptly made a decision. "No, no. Don't disturb
her. It was a personal matter. I can reach her at home
where she'll have a little more time." Diana, unlike other

women he was used to dealing with, had important things to do, a job she loved. He didn't want to be selfish and pull her away from that, even for a moment. His pursuit could wait until the evening. "You don't have to tell her that I stopped by."

"Are you sure?" Carla asked. "I'm sure she could use a break. She's been here since seven this morning."

"No, it's fine." Decision made, Marcus reached out to shake the young woman's hand. "Thank you for your time, Carla. I appreciate you taking a few moments out of your day to talk with me."

"You're welcome." Her smile was just about blinding.

He felt her eyes on his back as he let himself out. Marcus turned to look back at the building's plain facade that was not at all indicative of its interior, not unlike Diana. Then he turned to walk back to his car. As he closed the gate behind him, one of the young men gathered a couple of houses away called out to him.

"Nice car, man."

"Thanks." Marcus tipped his head in the young man's direction, then after looking again at Diana's building, got in the Mercedes and drove away.

Chapter 5

Diana unlocked her front door and walked inside, briefcase and mail in hand. She was emotionally exhausted. The day at work had been long—not because of the actual work but because the entire time she had fielded speculating looks and questions about Marcus Stanfield. It seemed as if the entire office knew she had left the Prism party with him. Or maybe they read the society pages, like her mother.

But no matter how much she'd told her boss, her secretary, even Trish, that the night with Marcus would lead to nothing, they didn't seem to believe her.

She dropped her briefcase on the couch and the mail on the coffee table and kicked off her shoes. In the kitchen, her eyes went to the newspaper she'd left on the counter. It was open to the photograph of Marcus and his father. A reminder.

She passed the paper and grabbed a pitcher of juice instead of the margarita she really wanted. Marcus. Even though she was determined to dismiss him from her mind, he crept into her consciousness again and again.

At work, as she sat at her desk going over the financial reports, the memory of his kiss had nearly overwhelmed her. His full mouth on hers. The hot crush of his body pressing her into the wall at Gillespie's. During lunch, while she sprinkled the packet of dried cranberries and almonds over her salad, she remembered the sound of his voice in her ear. How he had said her name. And the night. The night before had been plagued by dreams of what might have been. Hotter kisses. The cool sheets at her back and his muscled body at her front as he made love to her.

Diana drew a quick breath. The universe was a cruel place, she thought. Why else would the only man she'd been interested in in months also be the same one whose father had driven hers to suicide? Her hand tightened around the glass as she thought of her father, a powerfully built but emotionally delicate man who had left his family more wrecked after his suicide than Quentin Stanfield had with his trickery and lies.

The sound of the doorbell jolted her from her thoughts. She put down her half-finished juice and went to see who it was.

"Damn, I've been out here forever!" Her brother stood on her front step, hands in his pockets, a crooked smile on his handsome face that looked so much like their father's. "You have a man in there?"

In faded jeans and a T-shirt with a drawing of Darwin's ape-to-man evolution as stick figures, Jason looked very much as she'd seen him a few hours before. Full of energy. In complete possession of their father's wide-shouldered, copper-skinned masculine beauty. Unconquerable. Like he'd just woken up from spending the night with the gold-toothed girl he'd met in Coconut Grove.

Diana briefly wondered if she had been so optimistic about the world when she was in college. As quickly as the thought came, she dismissed it. In college, she had been worried about her family. About providing for them and making sure that her mother's emotional health remained strong. About the regret she had for going to a Miami college instead of the university in Madrid.

Diana opened the door wider for her brother and invited him in. "What's up, Jason?" She didn't even bother to address his comment about her having a man in her house. He'd only rung the bell once.

"Can I borrow your car for a while?" He passed her at the door, dropping a kiss on her cheek before flopping down on her couch and throwing his feet up on her coffee table. Right on top of her mail.

She looked at him. After a brief staring contest, he took his feet from the coffee table and dropped them to the floor with a solid thump.

"So can you lend me the car?" He gave her his puppy-dog face. "You walk to work every day, and the grocery store is just down the street."

Her house was on the very edge of a neighborhood that had been gentrified only a few years before. The explosion of high-rent condos, gourmet markets, eateries, dry cleaners and accompanying high taxes hadn't completely pushed out the original residents. At least not yet.

"That's not the point, Jason. What if I need to go to South Beach or something? It's not like I only go to work and the grocery store. My life is a little bigger than that." But not by much.

"I'm not saying you don't have a life, Di. Stop being so defensive." He looked around the living room and beyond to the kitchen, surveying Diana's place with his subconscious but habitual look of masculine dominance.

Diana went back to the kitchen for her juice and drank it standing at the counter.

"Just lend me your car for a little while," her brother said. "I might have my ride back by the end of the week."

They both knew his asking was just a formality. Diana could never deny Jason, or any member of her family, anything. Whether it was money or her car or blood. As long as she had it to give, she would give.

"Okay," she said. "But I need it back by Monday for work."

He smirked. Triumph in his clear brown eyes. "No problem."

"I hope not."

"Thanks, sis!" Jason jumped up from the couch, came into the kitchen and gave her a quick hug. Then he went to her fridge and rummaged through her kitchen until he found a pack of M&M's.

"You're welcome," she said as he reached on top of her fridge.

The metal bread box squealed as he opened it. Jason grabbed an unopened packet of cookies from the box and tucked it under his arm. Then he turned, grabbed a cup from her cupboard and got some juice from her fridge.

As much as she wanted to chide him for his rudeness and all the things he did without thinking, Diana couldn't. She helped raise him to be this way. He was the kindest boy in the world, but he took the love and everything else that she, her sister and their mother offered as givens, things that would never disappear.

"What's up with this?" He drank thirstily from the glass of fruit juice.

She put her empty glass in the kitchen sink as he pointed an elbow at the folded newspaper. It was turned to the photo of her and Marcus Stanfield leaving the gala together.

"It's a newspaper," she said, grabbing it from under his nose and tossing it into the recycle bin.

But her brother had already seen it. "Is that the bastard Mom was talking about?"

Against her will, she remembered how chivalrous Marcus had been, how kind. She bit her lips closed, wanting to defend him. Instead, she jammed her hands in the pockets of her skirt, turned away from her brother and walked out of the kitchen. The last thing she wanted to do was talk to her brother about her love life. Or her wreckage of one.

"The girl I saw you with last night was pretty," she said.

Jason had his mouth open, like he was going to say something else about Marcus, but he snapped it shut and paused. "I guess so, but she's a little young for me."

Diana smiled tightly, not knowing whether to be pleased or insulted that her brother's foray into her personal life could be so easily derailed. "Young? She looked like she's at least as old as you are, maybe even twenty-five."

"Like I said, young." Her brother shrugged. "I like—"

The sound of the doorbell cut off whatever else he was about to say. Diana went to look through the peephole. All she saw was the back of a man's head, the wide stretch of shoulders under a tailored jacket. This man was too expensively dressed to be a member of Jehovah's Witnesses.

She opened the door, and her jaw dropped in surprise.

"Good evening," Marcus Stanfield said in that low and compelling voice of his.

"What are you doing here?" She'd gotten his calls on Sunday, dying a little inside as she sent each of them to voice mail.

"I came to see you." He stated the obvious with a knee-weakening smile.

Diana drew a trembling breath. "I don't think it's—"

"Who's at the door?" her brother's voice boomed from behind her.

Marcus glanced briefly behind Diana, frowning. "Did I come at a bad time?"

She bit the inside of her cheek. "Yes. You did."

Diana sensed Jason's presence not far behind her, but she didn't want him anywhere near Marcus.

"When would be a good time?" Marcus asked with his charming smile. "I can wait in the driveway or come back. Whichever you'd like."

She swallowed and said words that almost choked her. "It's never going to be a good time."

His eyes narrowed slightly, and he tilted his head as if he thought he'd heard wrong. Diana drew back from the doorway.

"Last night was a mistake," she said. "I shouldn't have gone out with you."

"Is it that bastard?" Her brother's voice came closer.

Diana drew the door behind her, pressing her back against it and keeping her feet on the threshold. "I'm sorry. I didn't mean to let things go so far last night."

Marcus looked at her with an upraised eyebrow as unease twisted in her belly.

"What's going on?" he asked at last.

"Nothing," she said.

"Really?" A frown wrinkled his brow. "The other night you were into this as much as I was, but today you're talking to me like I'm a stranger. What changed?"

"She doesn't have to tell you a damn thing!"

Diana flinched as her brother's words exploded from behind her. She almost stumbled back as he wrenched the door completely open.

"Your father killed our father, that's what's going on

here!" Jason shouted from near her shoulder. "Get the hell away from my sister's house before I call the cops!"

"Watch your mouth, boy." Marcus's mouth tightened as he stood near the doorway, his body tense and angry.

Jason grabbed Diana's wrist and dragged her back into the house. Her stomach dropped at the confused look on Marcus's face. Jason slammed the door.

"That guy has a big set of brass ones trying to talk to you!" Jason jerked back the blinds to peer outside. "He's still there. He's putting something in the mailbox."

After a few minutes, Diana heard the sound of a car engine. Her fists slowly unclenched at her sides as she listened to Marcus drive away. Her brother rushed out to the mailbox and came back with an envelope in his hand.

"You should just throw whatever piece of crap this is into the garbage." He held the plain white envelope in both hands, about to tear it in two.

Diana grabbed it from him and shoved her spare set of car keys into his hand. Suddenly, all she wanted was for her brother to leave.

"Here are the keys, Jason," she told him. "Please don't crash my car."

He looked at her closely, noticing her distress for the first time. "Do you want to talk about this?"

"Not with you, no."

As soon as she ushered her brother out of her house, she opened the envelope Marcus had left. Inside were two tickets to the Alvin Ailey troupe's performance in Miami later that week.

She gripped the tickets in her hand, staring out the kitchen window with regret and anger creating a toxic cocktail in her stomach. How dare he approach her knowing what his father had done to hers? How dare he come back to her expecting her to be okay with it?

But remembering his face in the doorway as Jason had railed at him, she realized that he may not have known, for him she might have been just another woman he could talk into his bed. She smoothed the tickets out on the kitchen counter.

How had he known that she loved Alvin Ailey? She had been planning on inviting Trish and buying the tickets for them both but had to cancel those plans when she'd lent her sister money for school. Diana sighed as she thought about her family and her best friend. She picked up her cell phone and dialed.

"Hey, girl." Trish greeted her with laughter in her voice. "It's funny—I was just about to call you."

"Great minds think alike." She left the kitchen to sink into the couch her brother had recently vacated. "What were you going to call me about?"

Diana heard the shuffling of papers, then Trish's syrupy southern drawl. "I'm finishing up my budget for the month and realize I have an extra few hundred. I want to give it to Building Bridges."

Diana smiled at the idea of having extra money lying around at the end of a month. Her siblings, or even her mother, would snatch that money up before she had the time to even realize it. Sometimes she thought they knew more about her budget than she did.

"That's great, Trish. You know we're happy for anything at all."

"And I know you all could use it. I don't need the money, so why not send it around?"

Trish had had a sugar daddy who'd bought her a gorgeous rooftop condo on Miami Beach—cash—before he'd died. Somehow, he'd even hidden the maintenance fees of the condo in the monies paid out from his trust every month. All Trish had to do was live in the condo and be happy, which she managed to do just fine.

"Thank you for the donation," Diana said. "You know I appreciate it."

More papers rustled, then quieted. "What's wrong?" Trish asked.

"What makes you think something is wrong?"

"Oh, please. I've known you longer than you've known yourself. What's gotten your little panties in a twist?"

A reluctant smile came to Diana's face. "Nothing, really. Everything is fine."

"Oh, really? That's a big, fat lie if I ever heard one." She heard the sound of papers through the phone again, then keys jingling. "Keep lying to yourself, honey. But I'll be at your place in a few minutes."

Before Diana could say anything else, her friend hung up the phone. Less than ten minutes later, a car honked in her driveway. She rushed to the window and peered through the blinds. Trish's white BMW convertible sat in the drive, top down. "Come on, girl!" Trish called out as she waved at Diana. "I don't have all day!"

Diana laughed, both surprised and pleased. Trish must have blazed through all the lights to get there so fast. She grabbed her purse and left the house. Trish already had the passenger door open for her and her favorite neo-soul station playing on the car's satellite radio. Diana sank into the plush leather seat and leaned across the car to give her friend a hug and a quick kiss.

Trish looked gorgeous as usual in white skinny jeans and a gray blouse that dipped low in front, showing off her abundant cleavage. She had replaced the thick, waist-length weave from the weekend with a pixie cut.

"You didn't have to do this," Diana said.

"Like hell I didn't. You sound like someone stole your

pet parakeet and wrung its neck for soup." She put the car in gear. "Just sit back and relax. Try not to think too hard about what's bothering you."

With the top down and Anthony Hamilton crooning in her ears, Diana sat back in the leather seat and relaxed, as instructed. She simply watched the scenery of her neighborhood pass by—the couples walking their dogs, hipsters ducking into the corner coffee shop for an after-work latte, a lone woman reading something on her iPad as she waited for the bus.

The car rushed through her little neighborhood, south on Biscayne toward downtown and I-195 to Trish's posh condo. She sat in silence, her mind shying away from the reason she was in Trish's car. The convertible parked and Trish got out. When she joined her friend, Trish tucked her arm around Diana's waist. "A friend of mine sent me this decadent case of whiskey ice cream we definitely need to try."

They zipped up to the thirtieth floor and into Trish's penthouse.

"Don't say a word." Trish closed the door behind them. "Go in there and put on one of your bathing suits that's already in the dresser. I'll get the ice cream. Meet me on the balcony."

Trish was the only one who ordered Diana around. With everyone else, she was the caretaker, the mother hen, always making sure things went smoothly. But with her friend, she could just relax and *be*.

She changed into a bathing suit, then padded back out to the living room on bare feet and opened the sliding door leading out to the balcony and an incredible view of the beach.

At nearly 6:30, the summer sky above was still a brilliant blue. Bright and crisp, without a single cloud in sight. Sunlight made the decadent space even more beautiful, sparkling on the chrome-edged railing, covering Miami Beach in light. Trish was already out there, her gorgeous body on display in a white bikini with heart-shaped cut-outs at the hips. The swimsuit was strictly ornamental. Diana doubted she ever went swimming in the thing.

Trish had situated two beach chairs side by side. On a table between the chairs sat an ice bucket with a bottle of champagne, two glasses, and a thick towel draped over a pint of ice cream. Trish smiled as Diana approached, her eyes moving over Diana's simple, forest-green bikini. It was a suit Diana only wore at Trish's place. She would never reveal this much of her body at the beach or even at a public pool. If she ever visited such places.

"Sit," Trish commanded.

Diana sat down beside her friend, enjoying the simple pleasure of the sun on her skin, her friend by her side, the blue sky overhead. They sat quietly for long moments, enjoying the silence. They sat for so long that Diana thought Trish had forgotten the reason for her being there. Then her friend sat up and portioned out the ice cream, watching Diana as she scooped the golden dessert into two glasses.

"So," her friend finally said as she gave Diana one of the glasses. "Tell Auntie Trish what's gotten you all upset."

Diana found herself stiffening, or at least trying to. But the sun had done its work. Trish's uncomplicated company had soothed her. She swirled the spoon around in her ice cream, brought it to her lips. It was smooth and cool with only a distant alcoholic bite, definitely not enough to get her drunk. Delicious. Diana reached for another spoonful.

"Does it have to do with that hot piece of business you went home with on Saturday night?" Trish lay back in her chair and spooned ice cream into her mouth.

Diana stared at her. "I didn't go home with him!"

"But I bet you wanted to." She grinned wickedly and licked her spoon. "Did you give it up in the backseat of his car? Does he have a big d—?"

"We didn't do anything!" Diana interrupted, her face flushing hot.

"Because of you, I'm assuming." Trish's wide grin showed off the gap between her teeth she'd been talking about getting fixed for years. "That man looked ready to drag you off to bed the moment he laid eyes on you."

"That's not true!"

"You may not want it to be true, but I know men. And that man wanted you bad."

Diana felt heat move through her face again. Trish's teasing words burst the dam on the feelings she was keeping at bay. Her lower lip trembled. The spoon clanged against the edge of the glass as she dropped it into the ice cream.

Trish sat up and put her glass on the ground beside her. "What's wrong?"

"Nothing." But it *could* have been something.

"Don't give me that pile of garbage, Diana." Trish put her bare feet on the floor and glared at her. "Spill it!"

Diana clenched her jaw. "I won't be seeing Marcus again."

"And why not?"

"He's not the man I thought he was."

Trish raised an eyebrow. "I've heard he's as hung as Kwanzaa is long, so you might need to reexamine your sources."

"Not everything is about sex, Trish!" But she smiled at her friend's raunchiness.

"Then tell me, what is this about? Because I bet I know

more about Marcus Stanfield than you do. He's a very fine specimen."

Diana fought a pinch of jealousy at Trish's assertion that she knew Marcus. "Did you know his father is Quentin Stanfield?" she asked.

"Of course I did. All of Miami does." Trish looked confused.

Diana bit her lip in dismay. "I—I didn't."

Her friend shrugged as if to say "so what," her cleavage jiggling in the white bikini. "What does his father have to do with anything?"

"His father was the one who owned the factory where my father worked." She swallowed as the words caught in her throat. "He was the one who tricked Daddy out of his pension. He is the reason my father committed suicide." Her voice cracked at the memory of her mother on the phone the day before, sorrow in her voice as if it was just yesterday that Washington Hobbes died.

Trish shrugged again. "Not to be cruel, sugar, but what does that have to do with Marcus? Quentin Stanfield is a true corporate raider, but those two men are not the same. Don't blame Marcus for what he had no control over."

"I thought you were on my side." Diana looked at her friend in surprise.

"I'm always on your side. Encouraging you to get some action is most definitely being on your side." Trish winked at her. "You have to see how much nonsense this is."

"Not really. Mom called and chewed me out for leaving the party with Marcus. By the time she hung up, I felt like I'd betrayed my entire family, including Daddy, by kissing Quentin Stanfield's son."

Her friend pursed her bright red lips, looking impressed. "Damn. She's got guilt down to a science."

Diana sighed. "I don't know what to think."

"This is not about thinking." Her best friend gave her a wicked grin. "This is about you getting some serious man meat in your kitchen for the first time in months, maybe years."

When Diana opened her mouth to say something else, Trish held up her hand. "Okay, fine. Tell me what happened on Saturday night after I went home to my lonely bed."

Diana sucked on the inside of her lip.

She was very aware that Trish was surprised Marcus had gone after Diana instead of her. Another reason they'd been friends for so long was because they could read each other like a book.

When Marcus had approached them out of the gathering of elegantly dressed men, his dismissal of the dress code registering with her as sexy and even a little charming, Diana noticed how Trish had pushed out her breasts, pulled in her already flat stomach and cocked a hip. She didn't do anything nearly as obvious as fluffing her already immaculate hair, but as far as Diana was concerned, she might as well have. Then, when Marcus asked Diana to dance, her friend's jaw nearly dropped to the floor.

Diana had felt a small measure of satisfaction, although she hadn't necessarily wanted Marcus's attention for herself. After years of being the onlooker while men flocked to Trish, it was nice to be the one chatted up for a change. She was self-aware enough to recognize that.

"Saturday night was great," Diana finally said.

She told her friend the PG-13 version of what happened between her and Marcus, how her brother had called and cut the night short.

"That sounds like a damn nice date," Trish said. "And as much as I love your brother, I'd have told him to get a cab or something. There's a sex drought in your parts."

Diana flushed, remembering just how long it had been

since she had had any sex, good or bad. "I wasn't about to sleep with him on the first date, Trish!"

"Too bad," Trish said. She stood up and headed inside the condo.

When she came back, she had a decanter of golden liquid in one hand and a pair of tumblers in the other. "After that conversation, I'm convinced we both need the real thing."

She poured the liquor in two glasses and passed one to Diana. The fumes from the whiskey burned her nose. "Drink up, honey," Trish said. "This will be the last time you'll have something strong in your mouth for a long while."

Chapter 6

Marcus left Diana's house fighting his disappointment and chagrin. Had he been so wrong about what happened between them over the weekend? What they shared had felt so strong. So mutual. How could a day and a half have changed that? In the morning after their shared night, she was even more real to him, more desirable. He was sure she would feel the same.

It had been a long time since any woman had rejected him. It felt strange. Even stranger was what the man had shouted to him at Diana's door. His father, a killer? Hardly.

Marcus brought the car to a halt at a red light and lowered the windows to let in some fresh air. He rubbed a hand over his face, trying to decide what to do now that his evening plans were all shot to hell. His cell phone rang, interrupting his thoughts.

He glanced at the car's center console display, then unconsciously straightened his posture when he saw who was calling.

"Hey, Dad."

"Marcus, aren't you coming over tonight for dinner?" His father's voice boomed through the car's speakers, effortlessly powerful, like the man himself.

Frowning, he pressed a few buttons on his car's display to access his calendar. "That's next Monday."

He told his father the date, pleased Quentin Stanfield was calling to check on such a simple thing. Although he'd never doubted that his father loved him, it was only in recent years that the older Stanfield had begun making overt efforts to socialize with Marcus on a regular basis. This included planned family dinners, impromptu lunches, drinks at the yacht club. For Marcus, who had grown up regarding his father as a kind of demigod, this was a very welcome change.

"Ah," his father said. "Aliza was sure it was tonight even when I told her it was next week." He chuckled at some private joke. "Whatever the case, son, be here next Monday at seven."

"Of course." The red light changed to green, and he moved the car forward in traffic.

"By the way, are the documents ready for the Baltree Heights purchase? My lawyer mentioned it today and I told him you were handling it. I'm following up to make sure."

Marcus mentally reviewed his company's pending contracts. The Baltree Heights deal came to him almost immediately. He knew everything about the deal. At least on paper. He just couldn't quite remember the exact streets and city blocks that would soon be his. But he would fix that soon enough.

"Yes, that's on schedule," he said with satisfaction. "The owner of the last piece of property holding out there is meeting up with my agent by the end of the week. No worries there."

"Good. That area is ripe for development. I want to be sure we get in first."

"It's taken care of," he said.

"Very good." He heard the nod in his father's voice. Another potential crisis handled. "Good job, son."

"Thank you, Dad." Although he was damn near thirty-three years old, Marcus felt that familiar surge of warmth knowing that he was making his father proud.

"I'm sure you're about to spend the evening with a young lady or two. Go and enjoy your night, and I'll see you next week."

"All right, Dad. See you then."

He hung up the phone. In the silence, Marcus basked in the feeling of pride his father's words left behind. He'd always wanted to please his powerful father, even while fearing he wasn't as capable or as ruthless. Over the years, Marcus had built a reputation founded on his tenacity, fairness and ability to go the distance. Not quite the same as his father, who was regarded as a wolf in the business world. But one day he hoped to be as respected as Quentin Stanfield—and also respected *by* him.

Marcus tapped his fingers against the steering wheel as he drove, consciously allowing the warmth from his father's words to overshadow the dismay he felt from Diana's rejection. His evening was free now. What kind of trouble could he get into?

An hour later found him at one of his favorite clubs. It was early Monday evening, with sunset just a few minutes gone. But the underground club was far from empty. The lights pulsed around the room filled with surging bodies moving to the latest hip-hop beats.

Below where he sat in the club's VIP section, beautiful women writhed and flashed him their available smiles.

The music was nearly deafening, the base thundering in the cavernous space, the strobe lights like lightning.

Marcus sat in a wide velvet chair with his thighs sprawled, sunglasses over his eyes to protect them from the intermittent bright lights. He watched the dancers below him grinding their bodies to the music, teeth flashing in laughter as they enjoyed themselves.

At his side, Mario Spence, a member of his country club who he didn't know very well, leaned back in his chair while a woman gave him a lap dance. She was deep into it, and so was Mario. Her was back turned to him while her beautiful behind moved in tight circles on his crotch. She made excited little noises as she ran her hands through her butt-length hair and licked her lips.

Normally, Marcus was all about some action like that for himself, but the thought of a woman who wasn't Diana Hobbes touching him made him feel bereft, as if he would be settling for something inferior because he couldn't get the real thing.

He looked briefly over his shoulder and accidentally caught the dancer's eye. She winked at him, tweaked her nipple and gave him a naughty smile. He turned away and looked down at the stage, not even a little bit interested.

What the hell was he doing here? There was nothing for him at this place. The dancer on Mario's lap only made him feel even lonelier, more resentful.

Damn Diana.

She couldn't see him anymore? There was no way he had been wrong about what she felt for him. He remembered for the hundredth time how she felt in his arms at Gillespie's. The drugging heat of her mouth around his tongue. Her body's sensuous movements as they kissed.

The intensity of his attraction to her had made him nervous; she was nothing like he was used to. Just like when he got behind the wheel of his first sports car. Then he grew used to the feeling, even enjoyed it as it tore his composure to shreds.

Marcus looked over the crowd of gyrating dancers again. He was in the wrong place. Diana would never be in a club like this. Instead, she'd be at the office of her little nonprofit, saving orphans and getting awards.

He drew in a deep breath and released it as an irresistible feeling overcame him. No matter what, he had to see Diana Hobbes again.

Chapter 7

Diana's sneakered feet slapped against the pavement as she jogged along the sidewalk bordering her neighborhood. Hip-shaking reggaeton music pounded through the earbuds from the iPhone strapped to her arm, fueling the last few blocks of her three-mile run. Cars blew past her on the street, some going much faster than the posted thirty-five-mile-per-hour speed limit. Three driveways up, a woman held on to her Chihuahua's leash as the dog barked and tried to run toward Diana.

She ran past the woman and waved, sweat coating her face, dripping down the center of her back and trickling between her breasts. The music was bass-heavy and loud, helping to block out any unwanted thoughts about a certain man. Diana jumped when the music disappeared and a ringtone chimed in her ears. Panting, she pressed the button on her headset microphone to answer the call without looking to see who it was.

"Hello?"

"Diana, what are you doing?" Her mother's voice came on the line.

Uh-oh.

She slowed her pace and turned down a side street, away from the constant flow of cars. Whatever her mother had to say, she didn't want to get distracted by it and run into traffic. Accidentally or not.

"What's up, Mom?"

"I asked you first," her mother snapped. "Why are you breathing so hard? Do you have someone over there with you?"

Diana frowned. Was her mother really asking her…?

"I'm jogging." She clenched her back teeth. "What's going on with you?"

"Oh." Her mother sounded part relieved, part disbelieving. "I just called to see how you are with this Marcus Stanfield thing. You haven't seen him again, have you? I told you he's no good."

Diana kept her breath even as she ran slower and slower, soon coming to a brisk walk.

"I told you not to see him," her mother continued. "I forbid it."

The sun burned the back of Diana's neck as she walked quickly down a cement path, trying to keep her heart rate up and her temper down.

"I already told you I wouldn't see him anymore."

But heavens above, she wanted to. She wanted to dance with him again, to allow a beautiful night to take its natural course. She wanted to hear his teasing voice and touch him freely without thinking she was doing something wrong. But she also knew she didn't have that luxury.

"I know you, Diana," her mother said. "You always want more than you can have. Stay away from that man. Don't lose yourself like your father did."

"Mother, please!"

She was so tired of her mother threatening her with the idea of becoming somehow like her father.

Don't leave Miami because you'll end up lost like your father. You can't be the boss of so many people. Your father tried to be more than he was and look how he ended up.

Yes, Diana was tired of it all.

"Don't 'Mother, please' me. I know what that means. I'm only trying to help you. That's all I've ever done while you insisted on doing things your own way."

Her own way. She wished she was able to do things her way for once. That she was able to live her life without the specter of her father or the threat of becoming unhappy and dead looming over her. Sometimes she wondered if her mother had always been that fearful, or if it was after her father's death that she became so.

"Okay, Mother. Don't worry. I haven't seen Marcus Stanfield again, and I don't plan to."

"Just don't forget yourself, Diana. And don't forget your obligations to your family."

Diana sighed quietly. As if anyone would ever allow her to.

Chapter 8

The sky was a mixture of dark and bright, sunlight fighting its way through thick clouds as the smell of impending rain hung thick and heavy in the air. A storm was coming. A brisk wind blew through the palm trees surrounding the brick-lined driveway as Marcus firmly closed his car door and headed for the massive, Mediterranean Revival–style house where his father lived.

He had never felt comfortable visiting Quentin Stanfield at his new home. The Coconut Grove mansion was not the house where he grew up. It wasn't even where he avoided responsibilities as a teen. Instead, it was the brand-new house that his father bought when he replaced his first wife with the second.

He didn't know when his mother, Evelyn, had become obsolete enough for Quentin to put her out to pasture in a high-rise condo in West Palm Beach. He didn't know when their family of four had become something else. Evelyn in exile. His younger sister, Cherish, first off to boarding school and now away at a university in England. Quentin richer and even more powerful but as distant as ever.

Instead of the family Marcus had grown up with, there was Aliza Razzah. A former supermodel who had become the consummate trophy wife when she married Quentin Stanfield at the age of twenty-eight. They had only been married for six years, but Aliza acted as if she and Quentin had always been together. Marcus hoped she wouldn't be too surprised when his father dropped her for a newer model somewhere down the line.

Witnessing his parents' crumbling and oftentimes bitter marriage shattered any belief he might have had in long-term relationships. It didn't help that his father was a serial cheater and thought nothing of sharing tales of his promiscuity with his only son. Marcus never wanted to be like that. So he avoided women he thought would be hurt by him, dealing only with the easily affectionate types who knew exactly where things stood and only wanted material things from him in the short term. He never wanted to hurt someone the way he'd seen his mother hurt.

Thoughts of the type of women Marcus let into his life led him tumbling headfirst into memories of his evening with Diana. She was so different from any of them, so compelling and utterly unforgettable.

I want her, he thought not for the first time that day.

Then Marcus tucked away his thoughts of Diana, like a precious jewel, and rang the doorbell to his father's house. He waited only a few seconds before the heavy mahogany door swung open. He nodded to the uniformed butler who let him in and waited for him to close the front door before following him to the family dining room and adjoining sitting room where Aliza and his father waited.

The rooms were in an over-the-top style that seemed more Aliza's taste than his father's. Gold trim, hand-painted walls. Chandeliers heavy with crystal. Antique English furniture. A fortune in Turkish rugs. His sneakered feet sank into yet another one of those rugs as he walked toward his father.

"Dad." He shook his father's hand.

"You look good, Marcus! Who would have thought, a son of mine looking like a model for *Gentleman's Quarterly.*"

Marcus shrugged but was very aware of Aliza carefully sizing him up from foot to crown—his retro Jordans, True Religion jeans, pale purple dress shirt unbuttoned at the throat. The small diamond in his left ear.

"Aren't you just the handsome metrosexual," she said as she floated to him on a cloud of expensive perfume.

Aliza kissed him on each cheek. She was dressed for a cocktail party. A clinging black dress with a plunging neckline and a fortune in diamonds draped around her neck.

In direct contrast to his wife, Quentin Stanfield wore black slacks and a white button-down shirt. No cuff links. No tie. At fifty-seven, he was still a vigorous man. Neatly barbered hair frosted white at the temples with age. Clear ochre skin. Barrel-chested and tall, he looked more like a retired wrestler than a businessman. He exuded confidence and a good amount of bullishness. And that was just wearing his casual clothes.

"Thank you," he said in response to Aliza's earlier comment. "I think. To hear you two talk, it's like you haven't seen me in years. This is how I always dress."

"Except when you're at the office," his father said.

Which suddenly made Marcus realize that he usually saw his father in business settings. Either at the office or meeting up for a drink or dinner after work. Even Aliza, whom he had no reason to engage with on a business level, had often met with him and his father for after-work cocktails.

His stepmother smiled. "Whatever the case, it's good to have you here."

"Thank you."

"Yes, absolutely," his father said. "It's been much too long."

He slapped Marcus on the shoulder and steered him toward the bar, where he immediately started making scotch and soda with his fifteen-year-old single malt.

"Aliza has been talking about you coming over for days. She's been harassing the staff about making sure they had your favorites prepared for dinner." His father looked over Marcus's shoulder, and Marcus turned to see Aliza talking quietly with one of the maids, a young girl in a black-and-white uniform, complete with ruffled apron and pinned back hair. Something made Marcus think it had been Aliza's idea for the maids to dress like extras from the movie *Django*.

He cleared his throat. "That's nice of her," he said.

Marcus had never known what to think about his father's second wife. She seemed to alternate between ignoring him completely and fawning over him, treating him like the son she never had. That confusion made him not want to spend any time alone with her. Whenever she'd suggested dinner with just the two of them, he always declined. She blew too hot and cold for him to stand being in her company without a buffer.

He took the drink his father made for him and sipped. It was strong. He put it to his lips again.

"It's good to have you here, son." His father tasted his own drink. "I talked to my architect about the property in Baltree Heights. He has some really good ideas. The low-rise condo development is just the tip of the iceberg."

He looked at Marcus over his glass. "Everything is still on schedule, right?"

"Of course. It's just another deal, Dad." They both knew Marcus's history. Whatever deal he wanted and went after, he got. He was the ultimate closer, always with his eyes on the prize. "It'll be done in a couple of weeks, at the latest."

"That's what I like to hear." His father slapped his shoulder again, looking very pleased with himself and with Marcus.

They both turned from the bar at the sound of Aliza's carrying voice, telling them that dinner was about to be served. His father shoved a hand in his pants pocket.

"I'm very proud of you, son." Quentin didn't look at Marcus as he spoke, only glanced out into the room at his beautiful wife and the pair of maids emerging from the hidden door with covered platters of food. "If I had had a closer like you working for me, half the deals that fell through over the last few years would still be in my hand." He slowly curled his fingers into a tight fist. "And if you weren't such a success on your own, I'd convince you to come work for me."

Marcus smiled. "If my business wasn't a success, you wouldn't want me to work for you."

"Very true."

They both watched as Aliza made her way toward them. "What do I need to do to get you handsome men at this dinner table?" She put her hands on narrow hips.

"All you have to do is ask one more time." His father kissed his wife lightly on her bare shoulder. He looked back at Marcus. "Ready, son?"

"Of course." Marcus paused for only a moment before following his father and stepmother into the dining room.

For the dinner, he anticipated a delicious gourmet meal, courtesy of the Michelin-star chef Aliza insisted on hiring for every dinner party. Marcus also expected a few roundabout attempts by his father to lure him over to his company, as well as banal, slightly stilted conversation with his stepmother.

He wasn't disappointed.

Chapter 9

As Marcus walked to his car from his high-rise office building, the wind whipped at his jacket and tie, flinging the silk tie so hard against his face that it stung. He'd only had to run in for a few minutes, so he'd parked on the street instead of the garage, where he would've been sheltered from the growing storm. Too late for regrets now.

As he jogged to his car, he looked up at the overcast sky, dark in the aftermath of a midsummer rain, the clouds low and heavy with the promise of much more. He got into the Mercedes, started the engine and turned on the radio to check the weather. As if someone turned on a spigot, it began to rain bucketfuls, dropping onto the roof of his car in a relentless drumbeat.

For the past four days, as it had rained on and off, the meteorologists and everyone who looked at the sky had been predicting a hurricane. He hoped they were wrong. But the air smelled like a fierce storm, the skies that particular shade of dark with an eerie light pouring through. And the rain. The rain was as unrelenting as it was sudden.

The radio confirmed his worry. Expected wind speeds of nearly fifty miles per hour and the possibility of up to eight inches of rain. A tropical storm. Driving along the water, he noticed a few boats bobbing in Biscayne Bay, looking seriously in danger of being unmoored and swept away by the approaching storm. Days before, when he'd heard about the possibility of a hurricane, he'd secured his own boat. At the thought of the *Dirty Diana,* his mind wandered to the other Diana. The most definitely not Dirty Diana who had refused him almost a week before.

He wanted to give her space. But he also wanted to be sure space was what she really wanted. The meteorologist interrupted the music again to warn people to stay off the roads and to stay home if possible, at least until daylight. He wondered if Diana would heed that warning.

From what the receptionist at Building Bridges told him a few days ago, she was probably still at work. Marcus looked ahead to the on-ramp that would take him back home, then glanced further up toward 95 and Diana's office. He made a sudden decision and kept going north.

Maybe he was being stupid. Maybe he was chasing a woman who did not want to be caught. At least not by him. But he wanted to know for sure. Besides, a storm was coming. It would make him feel better to know she was safe.

The rain was coming down even harder. A fierce wind howled through trees and alleyways, rain pounding down onto the roof of his car, his wipers batting furiously against the heavy downpour. Damn. He really hoped she was already home instead of working at the office or trying to drive in this.

When he got there, he observed that her building was completely dark except for a single light shining through one of the downstairs windows. He parked close, then ran through the gate that had already been flung open by the wind and slammed in a frenetic rhythm against the fence. The rain soaked him in moments. His jacket and tie, shirt, slacks, skin. His Italian loafers were drenched.

On the porch, he paused, taking a deep breath of air after his sprint from the car. The streets outside the building were completely deserted. Not even an intrepid teenager ran through the streets for a last-minute candy fix.

Wiping the water from his face, he turned from the rain-battered streets and rang the bell. Waited. Rang it again. No one came. On a whim, he pulled at the screen door. It opened silently without protest. So did the solid door leading inside the offices. He closed the door behind him, calling out Diana's name.

A single light from an inner office illuminated the otherwise darkened space. The building was a ghost town, the complete opposite of the last time he'd been there. The phones were silent. No footsteps hurried across the tiles. The receptionist's desk was deserted, perfectly neat and tidy with only a set of business-card displays with the name and information of the staff of Building Bridges. Marcus picked up a card with Diana's information and tucked it into his relatively dry inner jacket pocket. From the hallway he could hear the howling wind outside the house, heard the *tap-tap-tap* of a tree limb against the building, the squeak of the gate outside as the wind knocked it to and fro.

He opened his mouth to call out Diana's name again when a slender shape emerged from an open office door. Diana. She was looking down at a set of papers in her hands as she crossed the tile floor on bare feet. She worried her lower lip between her teeth as she read, not looking up until she almost bumped into him. When she saw him, she squeaked in surprise.

"Oh, God!" She abruptly jerked back, eyes going wide as she recognized him. "Marcus! You scared the mess out of me!"

"There's a storm," he said. "I came to check on you."

"You shouldn't have bothered." She pressed the papers she carried to her chest. "As you can see, I'm fine."

Yes, she was. Even with the storm raging outside and the possible danger of the building falling in on their heads, Marcus couldn't help but notice how absolutely *fine* she looked. A plain white blouse draped over her elegant shoulders and the subtle rise of her breasts. The neatly tucked-in waist and flare of the pink and white floral skirt that ended barely half an inch above her knees. She looked like an ice-cream cone—cool and tempting. He wondered how she tasted. Marcus licked his lips at the thought, unable to stop himself from moving closer to her.

"There's a severe-weather advisory," he said, finding himself talking in the language of the meteorologist he'd just listened to on the radio. "That means you should be home, not here."

"I'm as safe here as I would be at home. My house is not very far from here." She raised an eyebrow, still holding the papers pressed to her chest. "As you very well know."

He didn't bother apologizing for coming to her house that afternoon. He wasn't sorry he had done it.

Marcus shoved his hands in his pants pockets. "Why are you being so stubborn about staying here? You could be hurt."

"Nothing is wrong with this building. I'm perfectly safe."

A flash of lightning illuminated the north-facing windows for a moment. Then a boom of thunder sounded.

Diana flinched and gripped the papers even tighter against her chest.

"Come on." Marcus made an executive decision. "Finish what you're doing and get your things. I'll take you home. I'll follow you to your house in my car if you're worried about being alone with me."

"I don't have my car." She said the words like a confession. "My brother has it."

The sound of a loud crash drowned out Marcus's curse. A shrieking noise. The roof above them shook. Then the whole building shuddered as plaster showered down around them. Diana jumped and another squeak of surprise left her lips as her eyes flickered around the room.

"Dang!" she muttered. "What was that?"

"It sounded like lightning hitting a tree." Marcus was quite familiar with the sound from when one of the giant banyan trees in his backyard had been struck a few years before. "Get your things. We're leaving right now."

This time she didn't argue. She ran in the direction she'd just come from and returned moments later with a large purse draped over her shoulder. Her feet were still bare.

"Come!" He grabbed her hand and pulled her toward the door, then yanked it open. Rain whipped wildly around them, flinging horizontal sheets of warm water in their faces and all over their clothes. Another shrieking noise ripped through the air. Marcus looked up in time to see a tree falling across the porch, slamming down, long branches flailing, dirt flying up.

"Diana!" He leaped back and pulled her with him toward the doorway and into the house.

They barely avoided the tree's crush. It sounded like a heavy groan, nature in agony as the tree crashed down into the porch, blocking their way to the gate and the car.

"There's another way out of the house!" Diana shouted. She tugged him away from the wreckage at the front door.

He allowed her to pull him through the house and toward the back. Thunder slammed through the air again, a startling clap that propelled Diana straight into his arms. He held her for a moment while she trembled, unable to move. Then she took a breath and pulled away from him.

"Sorry," she said, trembling. "I'm not usually like this."

"I think you're allowed at least one meltdown during times like these." He kept his arm around her, scanning the rear of the house for the exit she mentioned. "You ready?"

"Yes."

The storm lashed the windows. The winds howled and shrieked through the house. Diana trembled against him again as they moved quickly. She shivered as much from her wet clothes as her fear. Her clothes were plastered to her skin, her hair wet and curling up around her face. At the back door, they stopped. She pulled the door to open it, but nothing happened.

"Dang it! Nora locked the door before she left and took the keys with her. The keys open this door and the bars on the other side."

Marcus stared at her in disbelief as the storm raged around them. "I bet she won't do that again."

"No one likes a smart-ass," she muttered, frantically rattling the knob of the locked door.

Marcus looked back toward the front door and the impassible tree blocking their way. They had to get out of the house.

"I'll kick it open," he said, getting ready to do just that.

She put a hand on his shoulder. "No, you can't. It's one of those burglar-proof doors that you can't kick through. And even if you got through that, there's still the bars on the other side that won't let the door fall open."

He looked at her, his pulse thundering in fear for them both. "Why do you work in a death trap?"

Instead of waiting for her answer, he pulled her away from the door, fearing another tree or something else that might come flying into the building from one of the wide windows.

"I think we're stuck here for the night." Diana turned and looked over her shoulder to the other side of the house, a faint tremor in her voice.

Her words settled a hot awareness in the base of Marcus's spine. The two of them alone. All night. He spoke past a suddenly dry throat. "Is there someplace we can wait out the storm?"

"My office should be safe."

Lightning flared again. Thunder. Then the building went dark. Marcus couldn't see two feet in front of his face.

He cursed. "Just when I thought this couldn't get any worse."

"Stop tempting fate then," she said with bite. "Come on."

She stepped away from him, forcing him to drop his hands from her waist. But she took his hand and guided him toward the office at the south side of the building, tucked away under the stairs. He was forcefully aware of her hot palm against his. The rich, feminine scent of her close to him. His thumping heart.

The rainstorm and his sudden awareness of their isolation acted on him like an aphrodisiac, sharpening his senses, making him even more aware of her as a woman, of himself as a man. He drew a steadying breath.

As they stepped through her office door, Marcus's eyes began to adjust. Diana released his hand and walked away. Immediately, he felt bereft, wanting to pull her back to him, kiss her. His pulse drummed in his throat. In his groin. Drowning in his ill-timed desire, he could just make out the vague outline of her feminine shape in front of a closet door. Then a creaking groan broke the eerie silence of the room as she opened the door and stepped inside. She bumped into something.

"Sugar!" she shouted.

Marcus smiled in the dark, imagining her sweet mouth framing the improbable curse. "Why did you shout 'sugar' like a curse word?"

"Because it's better than the other thing I'm not going to say."

"There's nothing wrong with cursing, you know," Marcus said, glad for the distraction from his rising lust.

"I'm sure there isn't, but I just don't do it. I got out of the habit when I was helping my mom raise my sister and brother."

He heard rustling and more bumps from the closet. After another curse on sugar, she emerged with a mound of bedding and pillows in her hands. Or at least that's what he assumed she carried as she dumped them unceremoniously on the couch against the back wall. Slowly, his eyes were getting used to the dark, seeing details of the room instead of complete darkness.

"Do you have any matches in there?" he asked. "Any candles?"

Wordlessly, she moved in shades of dusk and dark toward the closet again, a slim wraith that captured his imagination and made his body want to move toward her. Watching her, the heat and hardness rose in him, a scorching and forceful tide. He tightened his jaw. A droplet of water slid down his nose. He shivered at that reminder of his other discomfort. With a low curse, he shrugged off his jacket and shirt. After a moment's hesitation, he pulled off his pants, keeping on his underwear. Already, he felt more comfortable without the wet clothes pressing against his skin.

"While you're in there, can you check for towels, too? It's cold as a priest's balls out here."

Her muffled laughter floated toward him. "I won't even ask how you know what temperature a priest's…testicles are." In moments, she emerged from the closet, holding a towel in one hand and a flashlight in the other. The light in her hand flickered on.

"Oh!" Diana froze.

She stared at him, her eyes traveling slowly from his face to his chest, skimming quickly over his crotch before taking the journey down his thighs to his feet. Her gaze scorched him. The flashlight abruptly clicked off.

"Here." Diana shoved the towel toward him.

He took the towel but did not use it. She was cold, too, wet and shivering in her flimsy blouse and feminine fluff of a skirt. The plain white blouse that had been elegant before was indecently sheer now, plastered to her skin and showing off her torso, her dark bra, the shape of her breasts. Marcus's hand cupped at his side from the desire to strip the wet clothes from her body and warm her with his own.

"You should use the towel first," he said, voice rough with desire. Although he might need it soon to cover the evidence of his lust.

He heard her swallow. "You're probably right," she said. Her eyes still did not leave him.

Did she know he could see her in the dark now? The finer details of her were lost to shadow, but he could see that she licked her lips as she watched him, touched a hand to her belly before taking the towel and stepping away from him into the closet. She closed the door.

Marcus drew a breath and rubbed a hand across his

damp chest. He tried to calm his thoughts and his want
and thrumming blood, but it was impossible. His entire
body was at attention. A single, hard ache. Just for her.

When Diana emerged from the closet, she only had her
bra and panties on. She dashed past him to grab one of
the blankets from the couch. Once swathed in the blanket, she offered him the towel. Marcus took it, brought it
to his nose and inhaled her scent. His body hardened even
more in response. Sweat. Her perfume. The spicy aroma
that was uniquely hers, like crushed rosemary leaves. She
sat on the couch.

Marcus dried himself, imagining the places on her body
the towel had touched. The ache for her became like a dag-
ger in his belly. He abruptly shoved away the thoughts of
her naked body and toweled the rainwater from his skin.
He focused instead on something that had been bothering him for days.

"Diana." He slowly rubbed the towel across his bare
chest. "What your brother said to me the day I came to
your house—what was that all about?"

She paused for a moment, the blanket gathered around
her slender frame. "Your father is not a good man. He…"
She swallowed audibly. "He deliberately cheated my father
out of his pension. Because of that, Papa took his own life."

Marcus wanted to ask her for more details, but he felt
her reluctance to talk about it, felt the trailing vapor of her
sorrow in the room.

"I never knew anything about that," he said carefully.

His father was not a kind man. He wasn't even a nice
one. There were things he thought Quentin Stanfield was
more than capable of, things he never confronted his father about.

"Sometimes I wish I didn't know anything about what
happened." She sighed. "My father's suicide changed ev-

erything for my family." Diana shifted restlessly on the couch. "I don't want to talk about this," she said.

Why? he wanted to protest. *This is the thing keeping you away from me.* "Diana." He said her name so softly that it was barely audible beneath the sound of thunder and slap of tree limbs against the house, the relentless rain on the roof. "I am not my father."

"I know," she said. "And I wish that was enough."

"Only you can determine that it's enough. I'm only myself. A man who wants a beautiful woman."

He heard the breath leave her throat in a long, trembling sigh. "Marcus. I think that…" But she didn't let him know what she thought.

He told himself that he just meant to walk to the couch and sit down next to her. Talk. Ask her to see him as more than his father's son. But at the couch, his good intentions evaporated. She looked up at him, her eyes wide and dark. Watchful. Her hands clutched the blanket around her shoulders, covering every part of her except her kissable throat, her face, that mouth he had remembered a thousand times.

"Damn…"

He dropped to his knees before her and she gasped softly. A wondrous and sensual sound in the half-dark. He cupped her feet in his hands. They were cold. He warmed them, massaging the smooth skin, the high arches, until her skin burned nearly as hot as his. Then his hands moved higher. To her calves, caressing, a leisurely journey to her knees, her thighs, parting the blanket as he went. He skimmed his hands over her thighs, her hips, her sides. The blanket fell completely away. Her hands fluttered down to rest on the couch on either side of her thighs.

He moved to her arms, caressing the delicately muscled biceps, her shoulders, her neck where his hand brushed the heavy wetness of her hair. She did not move. Only breathed beneath his exploring hands. He felt her breath deepen. The heat rise under her skin. But she still did not move. *He* was the one who acted, parting her thighs to slip between them, to cup the back of her neck in his palm.

"I am only me," Marcus said, feeling the words reverberate through his entire body.

Then he kissed her.

She greeted his lips with her own. A soft salutation. Once. Twice. Then a third time. Marcus felt a tremor move through him, echoes of the same powerful feeling that had overtaken him the first time they had kissed. Back then, he had wanted to ravish her mouth, to roughly share with her the lust she had awakened in him. But now, it was different. Gentler. Deeper. A hard sweetness rising in him, only for her.

Diana held herself still as they kissed. She only sighed into his mouth, caressing his tongue with the gentle movement of her own. But she did not touch him. She did nothing. It felt like she was waiting. Not for him, but for her body's permission.

Their mouths opened together. She tasted like carrots. And of the storm. She moaned and slid her arms around his neck, parted her thighs wider to receive him. Her breasts pressed against his chest, firm and inciting. But he only continued to touch her neck, lightly caressing the soft skin at the top of her spine.

Then she finally touched him. Pressed her hot palms against his chest. For a moment, he thought she meant to push him away, and he prepared himself for it, to burn in his unfulfilled desire and disappointment.

But she caressed him instead, touched the muscled hardness of his chest as a low cry of surrender spilled from her lips. Her touch destroyed his restraint. The desire jerked fiercely in him. Bucked hard. A leashed horse suddenly aware of its potential for freedom. His hand slid from her neck, down to her shoulders, then her back, un-snapping her bra.

He was hard as a steel pike. Throbbing urgently to take her. To give to her. To share with her.

Marcus tugged her down from the couch to the floor. She came to him with a low and lusty sigh, climbing onto him while his back hit the cool tile. She grasped the edges of his briefs, tugged them down his thighs. A hard shiver moved through him. His hands clenched on her hips, clasped her buttocks. And they kissed. Slow and gentle, the wildness in her growing to match his. Marcus could feel it. He held his own wild horse in check, waiting for the perfect moment to release it. She reached down and touched him. Clasped his hardness in her hot hands. The wild horse broke free.

He surged up against her, hungry for their joining. She jerked with his movements but held on, her delicate fin-gers exploring him. Marcus hissed. Then she blinked, long lashes quivering against her cheeks. She pulled off her panties.

"Do you have anything?" She asked the urgent question, her hand still hot around him, the breath coming quickly past her parted lips. He reached backward for his pants he had dropped nearby on the floor and pulled out his wallet and then a condom.

Diana took it and opened the packet with a whisper of the foil, her body a sensual darkness over him. He hissed in reaction as she slowly rolled the latex onto his hardness, her hands tender yet urgent. His neck stretched back. His belly flexed as she tended to him.

"You're beautiful," she gasped.

She lifted her heat over him, grasped him in her soft, hot hands. Through his sensitive flesh, he felt her pulse and his pulse thudding together. The tremor in her fingers as she held him. Then guided him in a slow agony of pleasure inside her.

"Christ!"

Heat. A vicious bliss. His breath stuttering.

Above him, she was a poem in the darkness. Her hair in loosened wet curls moving around her face. Shadows falling between her shoulders and jaw. Dark-tipped breasts, flat belly. The writhing mystery of her sleek body on top of him, around him. Her nails dug into his chest. Her neck arched back. The pleasure stretched between them like fine toffee, a sweet lasso that anchored him to the floor as she rode him. Her soft moans. The shadows moving over her breasts, kissing their delicate weight.

He reached between them. She gasped and spasmed around him as his fingers circled the hard bud of her desire, tightening the circles on her intimate flesh, pressing harder. Her sex clenched around him again, stoking his bliss.

Marcus swallowed thickly as the pleasure battered him, as she twisted, wildly abandoned and beautiful, on top of him. The room was thick with the sounds of their passion. Her breath. His breath. The storm howling beyond the doors. The slap of the tree branches against the house, the fury of their bodies moving in rhythm. Together, they were darkness and heat. Sweat and moans. Sighs and hisses.

Sensation whipped through his body, drew his spine tight along the floor, flung his hips up to meet hers as he was completely unmoored, unable to keep still any longer. He gripped her hips to thrust up inside her in frantic, hungry bursts.

His name fell from her lips in a low chant.

"Marcus. Marcus! Marcus…"

She moaned as her hands flew to her hair, fingers sliding over her sweat-slick face, over her mouth, down her throat, her breasts. The pure sensuality of her beauty shocked a reaction into him. A burst of undiluted lust.

Lightning flashed again, illuminating her body. Her parted lips. Sweat dripping down her face. Her breasts jerking up and down as she rode him.

"Oh, God!"

She jolted on top of him, her tight heat squeezing him even more as she gasped and shuddered, the rhythmic squeeze and release of her sex around him tilting him over the edge of his desire. The lust flashed through him. Completion. Breathless and electric, his body vibrated between hers and the floor as she cried out again and again.

Diana collapsed on top of him. Chest to chest. Belly to belly. She nuzzled her face into his throat, and her heated breath puffed against his skin.

The moment lingered into contented silence.

"That was…unexpected," she said a long while later, soft wonder in her voice.

He settled his hands on her back, tracing the sweat along her spine. "The best things are often unexpected."

She only breathed softly against his skin, saying nothing. Marcus's heart knocked in his chest in the aftermath of his desire. He wanted to lift her up, turn her over and feast between her legs, but already, he felt a distance between them.

Diana lay on top of him, her nails scratching delicately at his chest. But she might as well have been miles away.

Chapter 10

Morning. Diana could feel it more than she could see it. She heard the absolute quiet of the building. No AC. No ticks and flickers from the house and its various electronic devices. Only a faint rushing of wind from what she assumed was the broken front door.

Despite being fully aware of what happened last night—the tree falling, the storm, tumbling into bed with Marcus Stanfield—she felt calm and at peace. She was sore in places that hadn't been in ages, her body liquid and satisfied as she lay on top of Marcus on the couch. His heart beat steadily beneath her cheek while their legs tangled together in the blankets.

She shifted. It felt good. The sex with him had been so effortless. He had moved with her like a fantasy of lovemaking she thought she could only realize in dreams, skill and appetite coming together to make her moan his name, claw at his skin, spill over in delirious completion again and again.

Her entire body grew warm as she remembered the things they had done the night before. How eager she had been to feel him inside her. Still blushing, Diana opened her eyes and turned her head.

"Good morning," Marcus murmured. His eyes were a sleepy, dark gold ringed with black. Bedroom eyes.

She flushed again, looking away. Then she slowly levered herself up from him, carefully untangling their legs, separating the intimate nudity of her body from his. She sat on the edge of the sofa, using her arms to shield her breasts from him.

But he saw her. He leisurely took in her nakedness, then reached over to the inside edge of the sofa, lifted his hips and grabbed the blanket that had been trapped under them as they slept. He passed it to her with a smile.

"Thanks."

She wrapped the blanket around her body and stood up, looking around the room, trying to spot her clothes. Did she leave them on the chair? In the closet?

"I love how you look in the morning," Marcus said from behind her. Without glancing back, she knew he was still laid on the sofa, relaxed as if he didn't have anything else to do. "It's a sight I could definitely get used to." His voice was low and sexy, a seductive early morning drawl. Something that *she* could get used to.

"You shouldn't," she said. "I—"

A frantic beeping sound cut off the rest of her words. She jerked her head toward the open door of her office just as the thud of boots and raised voices reached her. Someone was trying to get into the house.

Diana shot to her feet, clutching the blanket to her chest. She didn't want anyone to walk in on her and Marcus like this!

"Someone's car is out front," a male voice said. "They might be in the building."

"Hello? Anybody in there?" someone else called out.

She darted a look at Marcus but he was already standing, magnificently naked, and striding toward his clothes on the floor. She noted his muscular back, the notches at the base of his spine, the hard globes of his butt, firm thighs and flexing calves. Diana swallowed hard, struck dumb by the sudden flare of desire for him.

But she had no time to pay attention to her traitorous body. It had already gotten her into trouble. She turned away from him and ducked into the closet to get her clothes. Marcus was already dressed and walking toward the front door when she emerged from the closet, still barefoot, in her wrinkled blouse and skirt. He disappeared around the corner.

"We're here," he said to someone she could not see. "There are two of us."

Rumbling voices transmitted the information Marcus gave, discussing the best way to get them out of the building. Diana crept up behind Marcus as he said something else to the collection of city workers gathered just beyond the fallen tree. It looked even worse than it had last night. The door was broken down by the tree's branches. Tree limbs had invaded the office, thrust through the glass and wood of the front door.

The reception area was a mess. A whirlwind of wet and torn paper, dirty water on the floors, pens fallen off the desk, the card holder and cards swimming in the small river running over the tile floors.

She turned, staring at the damage.

Damn!

And their landlord had just renovated the building a few months before. She swallowed her apprehension as Marcus peered through the broken door to the workers sawing away at the tree in a buzz of noise and activity. It was still raining, only a steady but light drizzle compared to the furious storm from the night before.

"Is everyone in there all right?" Someone in a yellow hard hat shouted the question above the rising and falling voices and shouts from outside, the stomp of boots on the porch, the steady growl of the saw through wood.

"We're fine," Marcus replied. "We just want to get out of here."

Suddenly, a crash came from the back of the building. Diana gasped.

Not another tree falling!

She spun and ran to the source of the noise in time to see the back door crack in two. Another blow, and the door completely fell down. A firefighter in full uniform and gear shoved her way into the house.

The metal door behind her hung open, showing the overcast day. Rain tapped against the stone steps of the small back porch and on the hard hat of a second firefighter stomping up behind their rescuer.

The first firefighter looked Diana over with an appreciative smile then glanced behind her. His partner did the same. Diana peered over her shoulder to see Marcus approaching. In his suit and buttoned-down shirt, minus the tie she knew was in his jacket pocket, he exuded power and masculinity, his eyes snapping with authority. The second firefighter, a man with copper skin and a smear of dirt across his cheek, smirked at them. His eyes moved from Diana to Marcus with obvious speculation. She dismissed him and focused on his colleague instead.

"You're not hurt in any way?" the woman asked.

"We're okay," Diana answered before Marcus could say anything. "Thank you for helping us."

"It's our job, ma'am." A small smile touched the woman's otherwise hard mouth. "Come out this way." She gestured for Diana and Marcus to follow her through the path she had created.

Diana paused. "Do you know how long it will be until we can come back into the building?"

"More than likely just a few hours after the power is reconnected," the woman answered. "Definitely not anytime today, but tomorrow certainly."

"Thank you," Diana said with relief. A day was nothing. She could take care of some work things at home until then.

"You should go first." Marcus stood to one side and gestured toward the gaping door and the fresh air that suddenly made Diana realize how claustrophobic the building had become.

"Just one second." Diana quickly ran to her office to grab her purse and shoes.

With her purse over her shoulder and her shoes on her feet, she climbed over the broken pieces of the door and outside into the fresh air. The firefighters helped, allowing her to brace herself on their arms as she climbed over the splintered pieces of wood and the snapped branches, leaves and twigs, and out into the yard. Her feet barely had the chance to touch the ground before Marcus lifted her.

She squeaked in surprise at the sensation of his hands on her, the warmth of his chest, his arm under her knees. She felt the gaze of the workers around her, but she was barely aware of them as her body focused completely on the feel of him against her, the way her breath fluttered in her throat. He smelled of his cologne and sweat, with the faintest traces of their sex. The rain fell over them as he carried her through the yard, past the fence and out to the sidewalk near his car. He carefully set her on her feet.

"Thank you," she said. "But that wasn't necessary."

"Those shoes are not meant for walking through a disaster area," he said with a nod at her secondhand, plain black Jimmy Choo pumps.

Only after he set her on her feet and she regained the full use of her senses did Diana take in the destruction around her. She gasped. The storm had done its work during the night. On the narrow street lined with various fruit trees, several trees lay across the road, blocking traffic. One house had its roof completely caved in by a massive mango tree with fat, ripe fruit still hanging from its branches. Mangoes were splattered all over the street while branches and amputated tree limbs lay on top of cars, on porches, even halfway through windows. Diana shuddered, wondering how her house had fared during the storm.

Amid the fire trucks parked in the streets and the city's vehicles with the Miami-Dade logo on the doors, she noticed Marcus's car. The silver Mercedes was relatively undamaged, only with green and rotted leaves sticking to its silver body, a few fallen twigs on its hood, trash and tree debris swirling in the water around its curbed tires. His wasn't the only car undamaged by the storm. All along the street sat cars placid and whole under the rain as the sun struggled to pierce the clouds.

"Let me drive you home," Marcus said.

Normally, Diana would have told him never mind. She'd walked the four blocks in the rain and high heels the morning before, and she would again. She had a perfectly functioning umbrella, after all. But the idea that she could potentially see her house like the ones on this block, half-demolished with tree limbs smashing the roof and windows, made her not want to go through that alone.

"Okay," she said. "Thank you."

They got into the car, and he skillfully maneuvered it

around the tree limbs and fallen branches and, guided by her directions, took her the short way home. The neighborhood near her office was the worst hit. As they drove the streets leading to her house, she couldn't speak. She could only stare out the window, fingers tensely clenched in her lap. She saw fewer downed trees, no ravaged houses, just small bits and pieces of twigs and branches. Nothing dangerous. As they neared her house, she held her breath.

The house was fine.

Diana released a grateful breath.

None of her trees had fallen. The roof was intact. So were her windows and doors. Only a few of the roses blooming in the garden looked battered as they bobbed their heads beneath the rain's steady drizzle. Purple and white bougainvillea petals scattered the length of the drive, but the plants themselves seemed mostly unharmed.

Marcus stopped the car in her driveway and she got out, her hands shaking in relief.

"Thank you," she said when Marcus came to stand by her side. Raindrops fell on her face, sliding into her eyelashes, over her cheeks. Diana fought the urge to lean into his strong form, to simply rest.

It had been a long twenty-four hours. All she wanted to do was curl up in her bed next to a warm body and not worry about anything. Maybe have some of the chicken soup she had left in the refrigerator. She needed comfort. She needed warmth.

But, as her gaze flicked to Marcus's concerned face, she wasn't sure he was the one she needed to get any of that from. Her body cried out its "yes" for him in so many ways. But her family responsibility told her to leave him alone. There was only danger for her in his direction.

Diana took the keys from her purse to put them in the door, but they fell from her hands. The second time they fell, Marcus scooped them up and easily unlocked the door. He handed the keys back to her.

"Thank you." Diana worried the inside of her lip. "I—"

"I don't expect you to invite me in." Marcus's deep voice rumbled in her ears. "I would like to see you again, though." He took a card from his wallet and slipped it into her hand. "I hope you'd like to see me, too."

Then he bent and kissed her briefly on the mouth.

"Get some rest," he called out as he walked to his car.

His loafers tapped against the wet cement as he walked away in the rain. Long after his car turned the corner, she could still feel the tingling on her lips from where he'd kissed her.

On automatic pilot, Diana walked inside her house, then closed and locked the door behind her. But as soon as the click of the latch sounded, she trembled. Leaned back against the door. A breeze from the AC touched her lips, brushed coolly over them, reminding her of the light press of Marcus's mouth against hers before he had walked away. Walked away as if nothing had happened, when she should have been the one to do that.

She hadn't meant for the night to happen. Diana blinked from her stupor. She dropped her keys into the small Chihuly bowl by the door, a gift from one of the donors to Building Bridges, and kicked off her shoes. But not meaning for it to happen wasn't the same thing as not wanting it to happen. Because she *had* wanted him. Even now, the desire for him sat in her body like bubbling honey. A rolling sweetness she couldn't ignore. It didn't matter what her mother said about Marcus. It didn't matter how her father had died. It didn't matter what her brother thought.

She trembled.

A bath. Yes. She needed a bath to distract herself from

Marcus and what happened between them. A bath, then bed. Diana made her way to her bathroom.

More than an hour later, she came out of the bathroom to the sound of her cell phone ringing. Trish.

"Hey, girl," she said breathlessly, toweling herself dry.

"Thank God! Are you okay?" Trish sounded like she was on the verge of a nervous breakdown. "I was just about to drive over there. I saw your office on the news!"

"I didn't realize we were big enough to make the news." Diana draped her damp towel over the shoji screen in her bedroom and walked naked to sit on the edge of her bed.

"Probably because yours was one of the few buildings with any real damage from the storm." Her friend took a deep breath. Diana heard the sound of liquid pouring. Coffee? Rum? In the background, she thought she heard a masculine voice, a low sound.

"Tell me what happened, honey. Are you okay? Were you in the building?"

"Nothing happened. Yes. Yes." Diana took her cocoa-butter lotion from the bedside table and began rubbing it into her skin.

"Oh, my God!" Trish screamed. "How can you be so damn nonchalant?"

"Because I got out of the building okay. The firefighters rescued us before we got hungry enough to eat each other's butt cheeks."

"Us?" Trish latched on to her slip right away.

Diana flushed at her carelessness. "Yes. I *was* working."

"I know you were working, but you're the only one in that office who stays past six. Who kept you company last night?"

Diana nibbled her bottom lip, reluctant to tell Trish but not wanting to lie either. "It was Marcus. He came over last night to make sure I hadn't been swept away in the storm."

Instead she had been swept away by something else. Pulled under and way out of her depth.

"Marcus Stanfield came over to *check* on you?" Trish made an incredulous noise. "I heard he was many things, but randomly kind is not one of them. What did he want, and did you give it to him?"

Diana's face went hot again. "He *is* kind," she said.

"And he got the punany off you last night." Trish said it like she was absolutely sure.

"Yes," Diana said softly after a brief silence.

That hadn't been what he'd come for last night. She knew that. His kindness had radiated from him despite who his father was. He had offered to take her home. Swept her into his arms like a princess in a fairy tale. Set her senses aflame.

"Girl!" Trish's shocked and excited whisper came clearly through the phone, as if she didn't want someone else in the room with her to know what she was talking about. "Was he any good?"

Although she had gotten more invasive questions from Trish in the past, Diana flushed from head to toe. She fiddled with the bottle of lotion in her hands, resisting for the first time the schoolgirl's impulse to gush about her night with Marcus. She wanted to tell Trish all the things he made her feel, how she had flown completely out of her body and mind with all the sensations he stirred in her.

"He's very good," she finally confessed, a smile sinking into her cheeks.

Trish snorted. She sounded like she was walking, cupping the phone to muffle the sound of her voice.

"Who's there with you?" Diana frowned, wondering why her friend was whispering in her own home.

Pause. "A lover. He's still in bed. I don't want to disturb him."

That was new. Normally, Trish didn't care about the comforts of any man. Especially when he was at her place. At their hotels or vacation cabins or Swiss chalets, she was her most accommodating, her most mistresslike self. But at home, she was boss of her space and she let them all know it.

"This guy sounds special. Who is he?"

"No one you need to know about," Trish said dismissively.

Now it was Diana's turn to snort. "You ask me all about how I spent my night, and you can't tell me who you were snuggled up with last night. Not fair."

"It's a new thing," Trish said. "I'll tell you about it soon."

"If you say so." She yawned. "Listen, I'm going to take a nap. I didn't get much sleep last night. We'll talk later."

Trish sighed through the phone. "Okay. Fine. But call me when you wake up. I want to take you to dinner so you can dish about all this good stuff. I'm intrigued. Finally, a firsthand source about the younger Stanfield and what he's working with."

Diana laughed. "I'm not going to tell you that!"

"We'll see."

She hung up the phone, still smiling.

Chapter 11

Marcus drove home thinking about Diana and their night together. He felt like she had been imprinted on him. Her scent. Her image. Everything. He'd never had a woman affect him so strongly. She called up both a protective and animal instinct in him. He wanted to save her from everything that could possibly harm her. And he wanted to devour her, take all of her into his mouth, his hands, his life, feast on her as if she would completely fill him.

He wondered what she was doing. If she had already forgotten about him. If she would use the card he gave her and call. Marcus couldn't remember the last time a woman had confused and confounded him like this. Usually, if a woman wasn't interested in playing, he'd dismiss her and go on to the next. He was not one for the chase. He had more important things to put his time and energy into.

But with Diana, he was a foxhound on the hunt, catching her wild scent in the air and running it to the ground. He had to have her. The memory of her thoroughly female scent against his skin made his heart beat faster. Her soft breath in his ear. The way her body had responded to his.

He swallowed and refocused as he drove across the bridge to Star Island and down the wide avenue to his front gate. He pressed a button on his dash and the wide iron gates eased open, allowing access. Aside from a small amount of tree debris littering the drive, his property looked completely untouched by the storm. The rain continued its unrelenting drizzle, tapping gently on the roof of his car and sliding down the tinted windows as he drove down the winding, tree-edged road.

Even after the long night with Diana, he was far from sleepy. It was time to get back to work. His secretary had already left him several messages this morning about meetings and contracts that needed his attention.

Marcus took a deep breath and prepared for his day.

Once in the house, he quickly showered and changed, then headed upstairs to his home office. Working in an office building was never his preference. Ever since he decided to go into business for himself, he preferred to work on his boat, at home, damn near anywhere except his luxurious office in downtown Miami.

He worked hard but liked to play even harder, using his money to get the very best out of life. Jetting to any corner of the world whenever he felt like it. Taking off at a moment's notice on his yacht. Partying for several days straight, his nights fueled by alcohol, music and his own considerable will. But as hard as he played, he also knew the value of business. Growing up at Quentin Stanfield's knee, he could never forget that.

When he started his business nine years ago, he made sure his research was thorough and the profit potential considerable. Now, Sucram Holdings was a multibillion-dollar earning company with diversified interests that kept Marcus's pockets flush and his mind active.

In the past few years, his father had encouraged him to try his hand at real-estate management, buying up land and buildings all over Miami and a few islands scattered in the Caribbean. It had turned out to be sound enough advice, with his father connecting his company, Q Stanfield Incorporated, to a few of Marcus's ventures. The connection wasn't strictly necessary but, although Marcus initially wondered why his father felt the need to join their interests, he had agreed. It was no hardship to work with the man he respected and owed everything to.

When Marcus walked into his office, a cup of coffee, still hot, was waiting for him at his desk. He nodded a silent thank-you to his absent butler then got to work.

Five hours later found him on the phone with his secretary, Irene. Her calm and precise voice came through the speakers of his desktop computer.

"That's it for today, Mr. Stanfield," Irene said, her warm Southern California voice swinging up with a smile he could almost see. They had been on the phone for the two hours, hammering out the details of upcoming meetings, making sure nothing had fallen under his radar during the past few days.

A beep sounded—another call coming through.

"Oh, one moment, please, sir. I think that's the mayor's office."

"Of course," Marcus said.

While she tended to the call, he gathered up the most recent collection of documents she'd faxed to him, looking them over as he prepared to sign them. After a quick scan, he noted the date and realized they needed to be messengered over to his lawyers by the end of the day. He made a mental note to let Irene know.

It was the final paperwork for the deal his father had called him about a few days before, the agreement to buy up a few blocks in a developing area near downtown. On paper, it was a good deal. Four city blocks in a mixed commercial/residential part of town that, once finalized, he would pass on to his father. Quentin Stanfield planned to knock down most of the buildings and begin construction on a mixed-use development he'd had in mind for years.

Marcus carefully looked over the documents, pleased that everything was in order and exactly what he and his lawyers had discussed. He took up his pen to sign his name when the address of the buildings caught his eye. A muscle at the corner of his mouth twitched. Something was very familiar about that address.

He looked away from it, his mind immediately supplying the image of a swinging gate, a mailbox, a tree fallen onto a once sturdy and neat porch.

Son of a—

Even as the shock registered, his pen was already moving across the bright white paper, signing his name and adding the date.

He was buying up Diana's nonprofit. Marcus looked down at the contract, then dropped the pen into the crystal holder on the desk.

"I'm sorry, sir." Irene came back on the line. "That was the mayor's secretary. She wanted to know if you'll attend the campaign fund-raiser they're having at Vizcaya next week."

"What did you tell her?"

"That you were very busy but would pencil the date in your calendar in case you were able to make time."

"Perfect," he said.

Irene knew how much he hated political functions. He tried to stay away from politics as much as possible, although his father always stressed to him how important it was that he cultivate powerful and well-connected friends.

"Thank you, Irene." He straightened the documents and put them in an envelope. "I have the last of the papers for the Baltree Heights deal. Send a messenger over here to get them delivered to the offices of Dillinger and Crane, please."

He frowned as he mentioned the lawyers handling the land deal, of two minds about how to go forward.

"Of course, sir." He heard her type something on her computer. "They'll be there in twenty minutes. I'm also sending the messenger over with a selection of ties for you to consider. The Brannon-Peoples wedding is this weekend."

Marcus smiled. "Thank you, Irene."

He heard the answering smile in her voice. "You're very welcome, boss. I'll get out of your hair now and let you get back to more important things."

He looked at his watch and realized the day was more than half gone. "You know just what to say to get me back on track," he said. "Once you take care of these last few details, go ahead and take the rest of the day off. With the storm, I wasn't even expecting you to come in today."

"It was just a little breeze and a baby sprinkle," she said dismissively. "But thank you for the time off."

"My pleasure," Marcus said. "I'll talk with you tomorrow."

He hung up the phone and leaned back in the chair, his eyes moving to the envelope waiting for the courier. He was buying up property that included *Diana's* nonprofit. Dammit. Just when she was starting to trust him, this had to come up.

The chair's leather squeaked as he shifted in its depths in discomfort. This was a good deal. One that had been too good to pass up. The price was right and the neighborhood was perfect for his plans. But his plans hadn't included Building Bridges. The house just happened to be right in the middle of the planned development. Right in the damned middle.

Marcus blew out a breath. What the hell was he going to do?

Chapter 12

A sudden noise woke Diana. Her eyes snapped open and the mattress squeaked as she sat up in bed. Disoriented, she glanced at her bedside clock. Nearly two in the afternoon.

What was that noise?

The light beyond her curtains was still bright, but her bedroom was sheltered in its own darkness. Then she heard the rattling sound again. She jumped up and grabbed the baseball bat from under her bed. With the bat raised to strike, Diana crept silently toward the living room. Everything was just as she left it. The day bright, the windows open to let in the half-light of the rainy day.

"If I was a burglar, you'd be dead."

She squeaked and spun around. It was her brother. He stood in the entrance between her kitchen and living room, drinking a bottle of mineral water.

Diana clenched her teeth hard. "What are you doing here, Jason?"

"Setting you straight." Jason drank deeply from the

green glass bottle, then dropped it with a thud on the kitchen counter. He was disheveled, even for him, his T-shirt wrinkled and pulled on inside out, one leg of his jeans rolled up while the other hung over his tennis shoes. "What do you think you're doing with Marcus Stanfield?"

Diana stared at him, not certain she'd heard correctly. "Excuse me?"

"Marcus Stanfield is a parasite. Why are you sleeping with him?"

She opened her mouth, but nothing came out. Finally, she just turned away from her little brother and dropped the bat on the sofa. Diana cleared her throat.

"First of all, who I sleep with is none of your business." She felt anger well up in her, but swallowed it. "I'm the older one here. You don't question me like I'm some kid."

"I wouldn't if you weren't acting like one," Jason said, his voice rising. "Stanfield is not good for you. He's just doing more to ruin our family and you're helping him, falling into his bed like all those other whores."

Diana drew in a hissing breath. "What the hell did you just say to me?"

She saw her brother swallow as if aware he'd just stepped across a line, but he didn't apologize. "How could you do this, Diana? You're betraying your own family. Don't you see that?"

"What I'm seeing is my little brother breaking into my house and talking to me any kind of way. Are you out of your damn mind?" She stepped toward him. "Again, who I sleep with is none of your business. Absolutely none! I can have Satan himself in my bed, and you can't have a damn thing to say about it. Marcus is just a man. A man who I happen to find attractive. Even if he is a mistake, he is my mistake to make."

"You're screwing up!" he shouted.

"No, *you* are." As she stepped closer to him, he backed up into the kitchen. Diana stopped. "Give me the key you used to get here."

"Diana—"

"Give it to me now, Jason." She held out her hand, palm up.

"Diana—"

She only stared at him, her gaze relentless, until he finally pulled the key from his pocket and dropped it in her hand. Diana curled her fingers around the metal that was still warm from his body. "Now go."

He shook his head, about to say something else.

"Just go!" she finally shouted, forced to raise her voice. "I can't look at you right now. I really can't."

A look of deep hurt flashed across his face, a squirming on his handsome features. She turned away from him, stalked to the door and yanked it open. "Next time you come here, wait to be invited in." Anger flashed through her body, burning into her stomach.

He stared at her, his mouth hanging open in disbelief. Then he gathered himself, straightened to his full six-foot height and walked slowly toward her and the door. "I'm telling Mama about this," he spat as he crossed the threshold.

"Grow up!" she growled and slammed the door in his face.

Chapter 13

Marcus held up the bottle of wine when the front door to Bailey and Seven Carmichael's condo opened. Bailey stood in the doorway, chic in a white sheath dress that emphasized the graceful lines of her body, her permed hair styled in an elegant pompadour.

"Marcus!" She greeted him with a smile and lifted her cheek for him to kiss. "It's good to see you."

"Thanks for inviting me. I was moping around at home before I got Seven's message."

Bailey laughed, a flash of white teeth against burgundy lips. "I doubt that." She opened the door wider and invited him inside.

Marcus had always liked Bailey. In the beginning, it was with the intention of bedding her. Now, he simply loved her as a friend. It was one of life's better coincidences that she ended up falling in love with someone he knew and respected, someone who, truth be told, was a much better match for Bailey than he could have ever been.

He stepped inside the condo, which was alive with laughter, the swing of classic reggae, voices of the other guests at the early-evening dinner party. A cloud of delicious scents drifted out, making his mouth instantly water. He hadn't eaten all day and had been very much looking forward to dinner with his friends. He should have been there an hour earlier but got caught up in a meeting that lasted longer than he'd planned. Then he'd sat in his office in the dark, trying to decide what to do about the Baltree Heights project. In the end, he'd decided to tell Diana his part in it and hope she'd understand.

"I hope I didn't miss anything good," Marcus said with an apologetic smile. He had texted both Seven and Bailey to let them know he was running late.

"You're actually right on time," Bailey said. She looped her arm through his and tugged him down the wide hallway into the heart of the large space.

The couple had sold the condos they owned separately to buy something bigger for the two of them. The two-bedroom, two-bath Brickell Key penthouse was ready-made for a possible expansion of their family, although Seven kept telling Marcus that they weren't ready for a child yet.

Although the building was all modern blue glass soaring toward the sky, the interior of their apartment was cozy and almost old-fashioned, with heavy cherrywood furniture, lush rugs underfoot and accent walls in warm shades of pumpkin and wine. The largest wall in the living room was a tall sheet of glass that afforded a stunning view of the city, turquoise water rippling under the setting sun, the bridges and boats floating on the bay.

Marcus counted at least six people gathered in the sitting room, all looking elegant and casual in their designer clothes. He recognized at least a couple of them, even caught a brief glimpse of a slender back that looked familiar.

"How can I be right on time if it started at seven?" Marcus asked Bailey, already knowing the answer. "It's eight o'clock." He teased her with his smile.

"That's because we always tell you to come an hour earlier than everyone else." Seven walked out of the small gathering to shake Marcus's hand, a smile at the ready. His accented voice rose above the gracious rabble coming from his guests.

The Jamaican artist was the picture of success. Marcus hadn't seen him and Bailey much since their honeymoon a few months back, but he looked prosperous and happy, a successful artist in his leather loafers, designer jeans and white button-down shirt.

"Am I that predictable?" Marcus asked.

"Sometimes," Bailey said with a light squeeze of his arm. She took the wine from him, a bottle of 2008 Colgin Napa Valley Red that he knew she liked, and disappeared toward the kitchen.

"Glad you could make it," Seven said, slapping him on the back. "It's been a while since you've been around."

"I've been around, you just don't see me." Marcus gestured to the elegantly fluttering Bailey. "You've been blinded by love."

Seven chuckled. "There are definitely worse things," he said.

"True."

"What?" Seven looked surprised. "You're not going to make fun of me for not having a harem?"

"The time for that is past, my friend."

Seven looked at him, a curious expression on his face. "What have you been up to lately?"

Marcus shrugged dismissively. "The same old thing,"

he said. He slapped Seven's back. "Come introduce me around before everybody accuses me of being rude."

"As if you'd care what they think." Seven laughed.

But he drew Marcus toward the living room, where all his guests were gathered. It was a motley collection of people—men and women mostly in their thirties, all with glasses of something or other in their hands, most of them swaying to the music pouring from the speakers, Dennis Brown singing about milk and honey.

Other guests included Bette, Bailey's troublemaker of a sister who he'd gotten along with the instant they'd met. He shook hands and kissed cheeks, repeating each name as it was told to him. He was exchanging meaningless pleasantries with one of the guests, a slender woman with a beautiful dandelion of an afro, when the doorbell rang. Seven left him to see who it was.

The woman with the fro, Alyx, looked him over from head to loafers with intent brown eyes. "You're not Marcus Stanfield, the owner of the *Dirty Diana,* are you?" Her voice was low and husky, a surprisingly sensual rumble from one so small and so old. She had to be at least sixty.

His brow quirked up at the mention of his boat. "Yes, I am."

"That is one of the most beautiful vessels I've ever seen," she said. "I had the privilege of being aboard her for the Tour of Boats fund-raiser last year."

"Ah." Marcus smiled. "Thank you. And thank you for supporting the fund-raiser."

"My pleasure. The young people's charity is one I always make sure to give to every year." The woman smiled up at Marcus. "You know, I—" Her words dropped off as she stared over Marcus's shoulder.

He turned in time to see Seven and Bailey walk into

the living room with a woman between them. His breath stopped. Diana.

Some emotion he couldn't identify came and went across her face when she saw him. Surprise? Panic? Disappointment?

Then his friends were bringing her deeper into the room to introduce her to everyone. She was gracious, apologetic for being a little late, moving through the room with the grace of a gazelle, the beauty glowing from her face and unforgettable body.

Bailey and Seven soon made their way to where Marcus and Alyx were standing.

"Diana, Marcus, Alyx." Bailey gestured to each of them in turn. "Now you know each other." Bailey smiled as she turned to Diana. "Marcus is one of our dearest friends," she said. "And Seven and I met Alyx while we were in Brazil last year."

From the look on her face, Marcus assumed Diana didn't want to tell Bailey that they knew each other. If she wanted to keep that secret, he would allow her to. He offered his hand for her to shake, saying nothing.

"Actually, Marcus and I have already met," Diana said with her slight smile, the corners of her full mouth tucking up so faintly it was hard to tell. "He and I attended a charity event together a few weeks ago."

"What a small world!" Bailey said with a pleased smile.

Marcus could only agree. He had no idea Diana knew Seven and Bailey.

After a moment's hesitation, Diana took the hand he offered. He drew her close, kissed her cheek and inhaled the scent of her perfume. She melted into him for a moment, warm silk, then, as if suddenly aware of where she was, she stiffened and drew away.

"It's good to see you again," he said.

"Yes," she murmured.

Marcus thought he felt Bailey's curious eyes on them but then dismissed it as his imagination.

A few minutes later, Seven announced that dinner was served and urged his guests toward the dining room. Over grilled lobster, vegetable skewers and garlic au gratin potatoes, they shared conversation and laughter. Around the table, Marcus made sure to learn their names. Alyx, the painter. Kisha, the makeup artist and good friend of Bailey's sister. Clive, Kisha's husband. The unforgettable Bette. And, of course, Diana.

He watched her in what he hoped was a subtle way, finding it remarkable that he should run into her at Seven and Bailey's place. Clive had just finished telling a story about a Harvard woman both he and his bisexual wife had dated when Marcus jumped in with the question he'd had on his mind since Diana had walked into the room.

"So, how do you two know Diana?" he asked his friends.

Bailey looked at Marcus with that odd light of curiosity in her eyes again.

"One of my clients recommended her organization as a good charity to donate to," she said. "I went down to Building Bridges to see what they were about for myself and just about fell in love with Diana." Her eyes flickered as she looked between Marcus and Diana. "Isn't she lovely?"

"Very," he agreed. "And so are you, Bailey. You know, the world isn't as bad as they say when good people find each other."

"You getting soft in your old age, Marcus?" Seven glanced at him as he handed his empty plate to the maid he'd hired for the evening. "I've never heard you say something like this before."

"Maybe I'm just growing up," Marcus said with a grin.

Seven laughed. "I suppose stranger things have happened."

The maid served dessert—banana ice cream over two fingers of biscotti in leaf-shaped bowls—while the conversation continued. Marcus was, of course, more interested in watching Diana than in anything the others had to say.

She was sitting across and two chairs away from him. But he was as aware of her as if she sat on his lap. His thigh muscles twitched at the thought of her that close to him.

He drew in a silent breath. Across the table, she appeared to be consciously trying *not* to look at him. She ate her ice cream delicately, and he watched.

Diana licked the pale cream from her lips, and he shifted in his seat. She stretched her arm to reach for another biscotti from the bowl in the middle of the table, and he ached for her to grasp him in just that way. He noticed the way her dress stretched across her chest, her side and the carnal curve of her ribs.

As soon as it was feasible, he left the table to go to the bathroom before he embarrassed himself. He locked the door behind him and bent over the sink.

Although he had no idea why she pulled away from him, he was willing to do anything to redeem himself and get her back into his bed. Or at least in a bed for the first time, where he could make love to her properly. Kiss her entire body at his leisure. Swallow her moans with his mouth as he rolled his hips against hers.

Marcus washed his face and hands, waiting for his body's desire to cool. He passed a quick hand down the front of his pants and stepped out of the bathroom, right into Diana.

"Excuse me." He grabbed her arms to steady her.

Panic flashed in her eyes. Her body stiffened against his touch, and she backed away from him with a breathless sound. He closed the bathroom door behind him, the hunter's instinct in him jerked to life with her recoil. The scent of her was strong. Feminine and warm.

"Diana…"

A low sigh escaped her. Dreamlike, her slenderness in the hallway. Her soft mouth that he wanted to kiss. Marcus swallowed hard as desire beat a heavy drum low in his belly. The voices that came at him from down the hall meant nothing. They were only background noise to the want thundering through his body, alive and primal.

"I missed you." The words fell from her lips like a surprise. She frowned, as if she hadn't meant to say them.

She bit her lip. White teeth sinking into the erotic pink of her mouth. The sound of her breath. His blood drumming. Desire and want were all he knew in that moment. He said her name again, and she took a step toward him, hesitant. Then another.

Marcus reached out and pulled her the last few inches to him, tugged her fully against him. She lifted her mouth to meet his. Wet lips. Hot tongue.

Her fingers sank into the back of his neck as their mouths deepened their connection. Tongues slid together, and soft noises came from her throat. Marcus reached behind him, grabbed the handle of the bathroom door, shoved it open and moved backward into the small room.

He tugged her in with him and closed the door.

Chapter 14

Diana was drowning. The pleasure pressed her against Marcus, making her quiver and move her body urgently against his. She swore she hadn't come for this.

She hadn't.

She'd watched him leave the table and head toward the bathroom with a kind of relief. The evening had been sweet torture as he sat across the table from her, eating his food and watching her with a man's hunger.

He hadn't been subtle at all. She felt her hosts watching Marcus as he watched her. Noticed their curious expressions after she admitted that they already knew each other. Since that morning he'd dropped her off at home, she'd wanted to call him but couldn't. The thought of her family's disapproval and anger held her prisoner each time she picked up the phone.

The days had been agony.

It was fine before she knew his touch, that quiet conflagration he built beneath her skin with his clever hands and hot mouth. But now she knew. And now she couldn't stop wanting him, even as everyone told her how much of a bad idea it was.

But she was tired of doing what everyone wanted. She'd given up going to college in Spain so she could stay at home and take care of her mother and her younger siblings. She had gotten a job right out of college instead of grabbing her backpack and seeing the world like so many of her more privileged classmates had. Her life after her father's suicide had been nothing but sacrifice and soul-deep hunger. And although being with Marcus did not nullify any of that, he was something she wanted and felt that she had to deny herself because of her family.

She'd wanted to scream like a petulant child. She'd wanted to drop to the floor and pound her heels against the tile, hurt herself in body as she was hurting inside, wail for what she could not have again. Nine days since she last saw him. Nine days since her brother had come to her apartment acting the part of a father who was long dead. Everyone seemed to be doing exactly what they wanted to do. Her mother had married again. Her sister, Luna, managed to earn enough scholarship money to go off to Yale while her brother thrived at the marine-biology program at the University of Miami.

Everyone had what they once yearned for. Everyone had the kind of life they wanted. The life she had sacrificed for. Now it was time for her to get something of her own. But as the days passed between that first morning and now, she did not know how to reach out to take it. Then she'd walked into Seven and Bailey's beautiful condo and seen Marcus among their friends.

She had been overwhelmed by relief—and fear. Here was the universe giving her a chance to get what she wanted. Now, could she take it? Could it be as simple as reaching out with her own two hands? And so, she had followed him to the bathroom. Reckless. Thoughtless. Her body ruling her.

When she had put her dessert spoon in the nearly empty bowl with a decisive click, Bailey turned away from her conversation with Alyx and looked at Diana with a question in her eyes. Diana only shook her head minutely and excused herself from the table.

The steps she took away from the dinner party felt heavy and significant. She pressed her palms into the fabric over her thighs as she walked down the quiet hallway where Marcus had disappeared.

And when he walked out of the bathroom, looking sinfully sexy—hard mouth, sultry eyes, his body beautifully muscled under the white linen shirt and pale blue slacks—something inside her imploded. His touch lit her from the outside in. A sudden fire. Fierce and undeniable.

In the bathroom, she whimpered under his hands as the desire rose higher in her. He pulled her away from the door and shoved her against the wall between the commode and the shower. She gasped as her back hit the wall. Her mouth opened to take more of his sweet kisses.

The pulse pounded in her throat. She quivered with desire for him, the urgency building inside her while his masculinity branded her belly through his pants and her dress.

"Diana, Diana…"

Marcus dragged his mouth away from hers, grabbed her thighs and lifted her abruptly against the wall. Diana balanced one foot against the sink, the other on the rim of the commode. He pulled aside the soaked string of her thong until she was wide open to him, a coolness brushing against her hot center. His fingers probed delicately, circled until she gasped and clenched her fingers harder in his skin.

He found a rhythm that maddened her, brought whimpers of pleasure to her lips. She gasped his name as he caressed her. Firmly, quickly.

Something pulled tight inside her. Snapped. Pleasure imploded throughout her being. She wanted to scream from the force of it. Instead, she clenched her teeth against the wailing cry that rose in her throat.

Suddenly, the doorknob rattled. "Is someone in there?" A woman's voice.

They both froze, Marcus with his fingers still inside her. Diana's foot slipped from the edge of the sink in her sudden panic, but he caught her with ease. She reached up and covered his mouth. *Oh, God!*

"Give me a moment, please!" she called out, her heart racing as much from the recent orgasm as the fear of getting caught having sex in her friend's bathroom. "I just had a little emergency."

"Do you need any help?" The voice on the other side of the door lowered in feminine confidentiality. "Do you need anything?"

"Thank you for asking, but no. I'll be out in just a moment."

"Take your time," the woman said. Her footsteps retreated down the hall.

She blinked furiously, pushing at Marcus for him to release her. He let her go, allowing her feet to touch the floor, moving back, eyes roving hungrily over her body, as if someone didn't wait somewhere on the other side of the door to ruin them both. Quickly, she fixed her dress, pulling the skirt down and the bodice up. She turned to see him coolly collected, pants and shirt straightened, breath even. Only his gaze was still hungry, lips parted to show a flash of white teeth as if he wanted to devour her. Diana quivered.

She twisted away from him to push open the bathroom window. He washed his hands, splashed water on his face, then dried his hands and face on one of the folded white towels in a neat pile beside the sink. Then he reached for her and quickly kissed her mouth. His eyes commanded hers.

"I want to see you again," he whispered urgently. "Don't run from me."

She licked her lips. "I'm not running anywhere."

Surprised pleasure burned starlight in his eyes. He nodded, then after another quick kiss, he left the bathroom. He closed the door behind him.

The click of the latch was loud in her ears. Diana pressed her hand to her lips and turned to stare at herself in the mirror. What was she doing? What had she done?

The woman in the mirror stared at her with pleasure-heavy eyes, mouth rubbed pink and bare of lipstick, hair a messy tangle around her face.

"Get yourself together." She had to say the words out loud to jolt into action. To wash her hands, press a damp cloth to her face and reapply her makeup. Only once she was certain she looked calm enough to face Bailey and her guests did she step out of the bathroom.

But with each step she took toward the other guests, the more she wished she was back in the small room again, falling away from herself as the pleasure writhed between her and Marcus, her body and his the only things in the whole world that mattered.

Chapter 15

Diana went back to the party feeling like she had sex written all over her face. But when she exited the wide hallway, no one paid her the slightest attention. The dinner part of the evening was over.

Kisha and Clive had migrated to the wraparound terrace to admire the stellar view of Biscayne Bay and the glittering Miami skyline. Bailey sat on the burgundy velvet couch between Alyx and Bette, laughing with her arm thrown casually around her sister. Marcus was nowhere to be seen. Diana put her purse on the side table and joined the women. They immediately made room for her on the couch.

Alyx's shrewd gaze flickered over Diana's face. "Did you put on makeup in the bathroom? You look positively radiant."

Diana fought down a blush. "Do I?" She couldn't for the life of her remember whose voice it was at the bathroom door. Maybe it had been Alyx. It could have been anyone; she had been so flustered and focused on Marcus. "I had a little stain on my dress I had to get out," she said.

"Come." Bailey gestured for her to sit closer. "Bette was just telling us about her latest clubbing adventures."

"Misadventures is more like it," Bailey's sister said.

The woman was pretty in a vintage pearl-gray 1950s dress that skimmed her body, the scooped collar modest and a perfect complement to her dramatic long dreadlocks and theatrically made-up face. "Celebrities are crazy." She named a rapper who hadn't had a hit record in a few years. "This guy charged into the burger joint and had the biggest hissy fit about being served over everybody else in the long line. I'd never seen a big man act so much like a bi—"

"Bette!" Bailey pinched her sister's arm.

"Sorry. Are we in mixed company here?"

Alyx laughed. "I think she's trying to spare my feelings. I'm not used to people cursing around me."

"Really?" Diana looked at her in surprise. "Weren't you raised in a family of artists?"

"No. Missionaries."

Diana's brow rose in surprise. Just then, Marcus and Seven appeared from the kitchen. Both men had drinks in their hands as they walked into the living room, talking quietly to each other. Diana couldn't help but notice how Bailey glanced up when her husband walked into the room, her face going soft with love. By the time Diana looked up at Seven, he was already turning away from his wife, a hand in his pocket, the picture of confidence and control.

Sometimes she wondered how the two of them had ever found each other. They were so different. But then she had noticed moments during the evening when Seven touched Bailey with an easy intimacy that made Diana blush.

They did nothing that warranted embarrassment, but it was her own imagination, seeing that simple harmony between them and imagining how that translated to the bedroom. But it wasn't as if Bailey and her husband had started kissing each other in front of her or emerged sweaty and postcoital from the bathroom. At the thought, she flushed again and looked away from her friend's husband.

But her gaze stumbled into Marcus. His heavy-lidded gaze, full mouth. The easy and masculine roll of his hips in the slacks that reminded her of how they had felt between her thighs the night of the storm. She squeezed her legs together and forced a smile.

"Baby." Seven moved to stand behind the couch near his wife. "Marcus just told me about his latest idea—a fund-raiser for Building Bridges."

Diana looked at Bailey's husband in surprise. "What?"

Marcus grabbed one of the heavy antique chairs and straddled it, bracing his arms along the low back. He looked at her, something in his expression both tender and conflicted. She glimpsed a trace of worry in his eyes. "I was just telling Seven what that tree did to your office the other day. Even though your landlord's insurance would probably cover it, I want to have a fund-raiser for you, something at my place, to raise money for the repairs and anything else you might need."

Diana didn't know what to say. Her gaze flickered to Marcus. She hoped he didn't feel he had to buy her something just because they'd been intimate a couple of times. She didn't want there to be any misunderstanding between the two of them where their business and personal lives were concerned.

"That's not really necessary," she said after a moment. "You don't owe me anything."

"Of course I don't." Marcus made a dismissive gesture. "But I want to do it."

With everyone's eyes on her, she had no choice but to

agree to the gift. Diana looked away from the brilliance of his eyes. "Thank you," she said. "You know the foundation and I both appreciate it."

"It's my pleasure," he said.

Their eyes met again and Diana tumbled into the dark gold for one moment, unable to catch her breath. With him looking at her that way, she would have agreed to anything he wanted.

"Okay." She sighed.

The rest of the dinner party passed in a haze of heated looks and wonder. They did not get the chance to be alone again, but Diana never lost her awareness of where he was or what he was doing. He was usually nearby and watching her.

At the end of the evening, she kissed the Carmichaels goodbye and left the condominium with Marcus. He walked with her to the elevator while Bailey watched them from the doorway. It was a long time before Diana heard the door close. Marcus pressed the button for the elevator.

"You're making me very happy tonight." He stood at her side, his body radiating a seductive heat.

"How am I making you happy?" She watched him from beneath her lashes, a tentative joy spreading through her.

"Because I want you, Diana." His voice was low and matter-of-fact. "I want you so bad that it hurts. After that first night, I never thought I would have a chance with you again. I'm glad I was wrong."

Diana swallowed, hands tightening around her purse. Well, she had asked.

The doors of the elevator slid open and Marcus stepped aside, allowing her to get on first. The doors enclosed them in the small space. He pressed the button for the ground floor and stepped back to the other side of the car.

Whatever she had expected from him, it wasn't this. He

was respecting her space and not responding to the hunger that she knew blazed from her eyes. Other things were on her mind—her family, the idea she might be making a mistake—but she wanted him, too. "I want to take you away," he said. "Will you come with me?"

For a moment, Diana allowed herself to imagine that she could say yes. Running away with him and leaving all her responsibilities behind was such a fantasy that it was impossible.

"I can't," she said. "I wish I could, but I just have too many things to take care of here."

After a moment, he tilted his head in acceptance. "All right, but one day I'm going to get you all to myself. And I won't let you go."

Chapter 16

Marcus leaned on the railing at the top of the staircase, watching the ballroom below him quickly fill with some of Miami's richest and most generous residents. At this celebration of the Building Bridges and the woman who had helped to make it what it was, Marcus was only there for Diana, and he was waiting patiently for her to arrive.

After that heated evening at the Carmichaels', he'd dreamed of her every night, wondered what it would have been like to have her for the entire weekend at a hotel somewhere or maybe on a boat. Just the two of them indulging their senses in each other. He vowed that one day he would make that fantasy a reality.

He drew a calming breath and turned his attention back to the ballroom.

A five-piece jazz band played Louis Armstrong from the raised platform at the front of the room just beneath the stairs, while the crystal chandelier threw shards of light over the gathered company in their cocktail dresses and sports jackets. In the center of the room, a large, cut-crystal box stood on a pedestal, waiting to be filled with money.

Diana's boss from Building Bridges was already at the party and was vocally excited about the fund-raiser and the party's guest list. Diana, however, was obviously a little suspicious of why Marcus had planned the event.

He had battled with himself over what he wanted from her and even what she thought of him. He'd never had these thoughts about any other woman. But that internal war hadn't made things any clearer. He didn't believe in lasting relationships now any more than he did a few weeks ago when he'd first met her, but he knew that he wanted her in his life. She was becoming too precious to him. Too necessary.

And that thought frightened him. It made him want to pull away from her and send her back to her straitlaced world and pretend they had never met. It would have been easier if she'd been just like the others—focused on his money and on what he could give her. But she didn't seem to give a damn that he was worth billions, that he could buy her the city if that was what she wanted.

Some sixth sense made him lift his head as the butler escorted another guest into the party from the foyer. He saw Diana walk into his house to the slow and rousing music of Claire de Lune. She smiled politely at the butler, though Marcus could see the trepidation in her face.

She was wearing another of her vintage designer dresses. This one was yellow and high-necked and clung to her slim hips like a dream, the hem ending just below her knees. A white belt hugged her slender waist and she carried a small white clutch as her only other accessory. She walked into the ballroom, her steps graceful but hesitant.

Within moments, she found her boss and a woman he didn't recognize. But she didn't stay with them for long.

She wove through the room, greeting the billionaires as respectfully as their paid escorts, along with the community organizers and reporters, treating each person to a stretch of her soft lips, a strong handshake and solid eye contact as they spoke with her.

Marcus's body tightened with each step Diana took. He had brought her to his home to reveal what he was about to do with Baltree Heights, to soften the blow with the money from the fund-raiser. But as he watched her, all he could think about was making love to her again, pressing that slim and responsive body against his and making her cry out his name until they were both satisfied.

It was at that moment that she looked up and saw him. He noticed that her body softened at the sight of him, that her hands clenched around the small leather clutch. He felt her eyes roam up his body from the tips of his shoes to his crown, lingering on his tailored black slacks, the white shirt and black dinner jacket. Only when she met his eyes did he begin the slow journey down the long staircase to the ballroom below.

"Diana." He called her name softly as he descended the stairs to greet her. More than one person stopped to watch him go to her. Diana's face darkened in embarrassment from the attention, but she did not pull back when he brushed his cheek to hers in welcome. She smelled like roses and mint leaves, feminine and refreshing.

The desire he had for her was something beyond his control. He wanted her like he'd never wanted another woman, and he wished she'd come to him for the pleasure he had in store for them both. But he also knew that the way she fought him was as integral to their dance as the perfect way their bodies fit together.

"You're just in time," he said.

The party had started at seven, and it was almost eight.

"Am I, Marcus?" She said his name, and all he remembered were the moments between them in the Carmichaels' bathroom, her fingers gripping the back of his neck as he brought her pleasure.

He cleared his throat. "I was just about to make an announcement about the fund-raiser," he said.

"Oh, good," she murmured.

He touched her again, unable to help himself. Did he imagine it, or did she relax into him just a little? A smile curved the corner of her mouth. He cleared his throat and left her for the front of the room, where the band was moving into the final strains of "Stormy Weather." He gave a signal to the lead singer, a voluptuous woman in a clinging black dress, who led the band down-tempo and then to a graceful stop.

Marcus stood on the raised platform with the band as the conversations dropped to a hush, then stopped altogether.

"Thank you all very much for coming here tonight," he said, raising his voice.

The crowd looked at him with a mixture of curiosity and interest. "I know there are other things you could be doing on a Friday evening, but I'm very pleased you decided to spend it here for this wonderful cause that is Building Bridges, Miami."

"You know we come any time you call, Marcus," Letisha McBride, a pretty woman in a white dress, said. She was pouty and gorgeous in a way that was forgettable in Miami.

A few titters sounded through the crowd. They knew enough about Letty and Marcus's past that they were amused she still came around and considered him one of her acquaintances.

He smiled graciously in her direction. "Thanks, Letty."

He couldn't help but glance toward Diana. She was looking at Letty with a narrowed gaze.

"I won't stand up here and bore you any longer," he said. "Enjoy yourself tonight. My staff will offer you everything you need to have a good time. Just make sure you give generously before you go." He pointed to the silver box in the center of the large room. "Thank you all again for coming."

He left the platform to their applause, then nodded at the band to continue. They immediately launched into "The Lady is a Tramp," which drew even more laughter.

Letty McBride found Marcus immediately. She squeezed his shoulders through the jacket, her gaze measuring and admiring. "Thanks again for the invite, handsome. It was a nice surprise. You, having a fund-raiser? Will wonders never cease?" Her brown eyes danced in her narrow, vulpine face. "Next you'll be adopting some of these kids yourself."

She definitely didn't know him as well as she thought. Marcus pulled away from Letty as soon as he could without seeming rude. She was a woman he had once dated briefly, years ago. But even though her family had a significant amount of money and influence in Miami, their coffers were running dry thanks to her father's bad management of the family funds. Since his investments had begun doing well, Letty had tried to come back into his life, making it obvious she wants to lure him to the altar.

But Marcus wasn't interested in a convenient marriage. He wasn't interested in marriage at all.

"You never know, Letty," he said in reply to her comment about him adopting kids. "People change and develop new interests."

From the corner of his eye, he saw Diana walking toward the crystal donation box with the unknown woman from her office, a short redhead in a green dress. The large box was more than three-quarters full and getting fuller by the hour. After a brief squeeze of Letty's hand, he excused himself to go to Diana. He grabbed two glasses of champagne from a passing waiter on the way.

"I can't believe this party," the woman with Diana said. "Isn't it great? This will probably be our best fund-raiser for the year."

Diana eyed the crystal box filled with folded checks and cash as if it were a coffin. "Even if the box doesn't get any fuller than this, Nora will be very happy." She shifted from one hip to the other, her bottom rolling seductively under the yellow silk. Marcus swallowed.

"Ladies." He approached the women with a smile, offering each a glass of champagne.

"Thank you." The woman at Diana's side eyed the golden liquid but did not take the glass. "But I don't drink champagne. You should share it with Diana." Her smile was positively wicked. "Enjoy. I'm going to see what else is around here to eat." She sauntered off, waving at them over her shoulder.

Diana absently took the champagne even as she gave the woman a narrow-eyed, suspicious gaze. "What is going on with everyone in my office tonight?"

"Maybe she was just hungry?" He shrugged.

Diana's eyes met his. Then she took a sip of the champagne. "Thank you."

"It's my pleasure." He held his glass in his hand without sipping from it, drinking up the sight of her instead, the upswept hair and the delicate tendrils at her temples, the luscious deep burgundy shade of her lips.

They stared at each other in silence while the music played, the hip-shaking jazz and lights from the chandelier lending a particularly sharp and luminous air to the evening—and to Diana. She was easily the most captivating woman he'd ever met.

She cleared her throat, making him suddenly aware of just how hungrily he had been staring at her. "Your house…it looks wonderful."

"Thank you." He watched as she licked her lips, her pink tongue against her plump red mouth. Marcus took a conscious step back from the temptation of her. "Would you like a tour?"

She looked surprised. "Sure. That would be nice."

He took her elbow and guided her through the crowded ballroom, past people who looked at them with more than idle curiosity. Marcus nodded to them all, pausing to greet or introduce Diana to some as they made their way through the crowd and to the stairs.

"You know a lot of people" she said.

He smiled. "It's part of my job."

Their footsteps sounded against the polished wood of the curving stairs as he walked behind her. Her hair smelled like flowers, the scent of it trailing in her wake as she moved ahead of him, graceful and delicate with her hand on the banister. They climbed higher, leaving the sound of conversations behind. Everything became an aural blur. Only the music floated above it all, trumpeting and cheerful with the singer's voice rising above the instruments.

As they arrived on the landing, she drew a soft breath of appreciation. Marcus stopped behind her, admiring the line of her back and the curve of her hips while she looked down at the ballroom with the lights, the band, the wide windows with a view of the tropical garden and manicured grounds.

"Such a gorgeous place," she said.

"Thank you. I pay the very best to make sure it stays that way."

She turned to look at him over her shoulder. "You're definitely getting your money's worth," she said. "Show me the rest."

With that look, he knew that Diana wanted him. But he knew that a woman like her needed more than the pounding of the blood and the burst of desire between two people to invest herself, to trust. And he wanted her trust, even as he knew that once he told her he was about to buy Baltree Heights from under her, she would be furious.

Marcus cleared his throat. He took her through the rest of the twenty-two-room mansion, finally ending up in one of his favorite places in the house, a glassed-in room with a view of Biscayne Bay and the city of Miami. It was where he practiced his tai chi each morning, an exercise that centered his mind in the midst of the controlled chaos his life sometimes became.

"Where is this?" Diana turned to face the stained glass windows taking up a third of the east-facing wall, a large, three-paneled rendering of Marrakesh, a panorama of the city spread out under a wide, amber sky, featuring the turrets of the Koutoubia Mosque.

It was an awe-inspiring piece, each portion of glass perfectly capturing any light at any time of the day. Now, night lights on the floor illuminated the triptych from below, making the ancient city glow in shades of amber, carnelian and gold. He'd bought it on one of his trips to Morocco, paying to ship the large sections of glass from the other side of the world and installed by the artist in his home. It had been worth every penny.

"It's one of my favorite cities," he told Diana as she put the glass of champagne to her lips. "It's the first place my father took me to that really impressed me. At the time, I had no idea how to articulate what I found so fascinating, but now as an adult, I can say that I love the sense of history of the city, the beauty and the deep spirituality you sense in every corner."

He put his glass of champagne on the floor and came to stand behind her, inhaling the scent of her hair and feeling the rightness of her being in his home with him.

"It's lovely." She leaned back, resting against him, her hair brushing his cheek. "I've never really been anywhere."

He watched their faint reflection in the glass, her delicate loveliness and the way she seemed to fit so perfectly against him.

"When I was a little girl," Diana said, "I always wanted to travel. I watched all the documentaries on PBS and dreamed of the amazing places I would visit. I planned for a life of traveling. I wanted it so much." She bit her lip and looked away to the wall of the plane, then back to the glass of champagne in front of her. "But my father died, and everything changed."

The silence sat between them for a moment. Marcus thought of several things to say, but they all seemed inadequate. Instead, he touched her arms, keeping her in an open embrace.

"Can you tell me what happened?" he asked.

She stared at him in the glass. "You mean you don't know?"

"Why should I?"

Her body stiffened against him. "Does your father cheat and ruin so many men every year that they're all a blur?" The words dripped from her lips, poisonous. Pained.

Marcus flinched from her hurt. "My father is his own man. He doesn't share many of his business decisions with me." He lightly squeezed her arms. "Tell me what happened. Please."

She trembled against him. "I know what happened to my father wasn't your fault. It's just that my entire family suffered so much afterward. Daddy was dead, and Mama couldn't get his pension. It was hard keeping perspective knowing Quentin Stanfield was off enjoying his rich life when we could barely put food on the table, and I had to give up going to school in Spain just so my family wouldn't starve."

Diana blew out a harsh breath. "Sorry."

"You don't have anything to apologize for," Marcus said.

He couldn't imagine what she must have been through. Losing a parent. Watching all her dreams dry up in front of her face just because of one man.

"Daddy…Daddy had always been a delicate man." She continued as if he hadn't spoken. "Not the look of him but his constitution, you could call it. Science would probably say that he suffered from depression most of his life and didn't get treated for it in time." She toyed with the champagne flute in her hand but did not drink from it.

"He didn't have many friends, and his family was everything to him. He preferred his life to be simple. He was happy to work at the same plant for nearly twenty years. The paycheck was steady, the insurance was decent, and the factory was only a few miles from home."

Diana's voice sagged as she talked about a life that could have easily been Marcus's. In another reality, if things had turned out even a little differently. Three children, an adoring wife and a rented three-bedroom house that was comfortable for all of them.

Then, her father started forgetting things he had easily remembered before. He began to weaken. After several visits to the doctor, they decided that he should retire. Drawing his pension wouldn't require his wife to make any significant changes to their lives. The money would be less than his current salary, but it would be enough to carry them through. Diana would have to pay for college herself, something she had expected to do anyway.

But when Washington Hobbes approached his boss about retiring, the man was hesitant at first, then said he would talk to his own boss about the options. They agreed he would retire, and they agreed on the amount of his pension. Then one day he came home and said he had been fired for job performance just a few weeks before his pension eligibility date. The whole family was stunned. Her father was devastated.

No one knew where he got a gun. One night he went down to the river where he often took his children fishing. There, he shot himself in the head, his body pitching face-first into the water, where Diana's mother later found him.

"Mom told us how he looked floating there in the water, his body bloated and gray, almost unrecognizable with the back of his head completely gone." Diana trembled again. "I couldn't stand being in water after that."

Marcus winced, easily imagining the putrefying corpse and the filthy water around it. A young girl with a vivid imagination and a mother who didn't know any better to spare her children the details of her husband's gruesome suicide.

"I was so mad at him." Diana looked up at Marcus, a flash of that long-gone anger in her brown eyes. "How could he have been so selfish knowing that we needed him?" She bit her lip. "My mother had to get another job. I had to start working to help out. My childhood ended."

Diana shook herself. "I didn't want to talk about this. It's old but still raw."

"Something like that will never stop hurting," Marcus said. "Your entire life changed."

"Yes, it did."

What she did not say, but that he could see plainly on her face, was that she'd changed, too. He saw hints of the girl who used to laugh. The child who did not have a mountain of responsibility dropped onto her narrow shoulders. A young woman who had smiled with her whole face and body instead of the reserved tilt of lips she gave now.

Marcus wanted to rescue that smiling girl from the cupboard where she had been shut. He wanted to see her and Diana become one.

"Your father would be proud of the woman you've become," he said, "in spite of all you've been through."

In the glass, he saw her trembling smile, how she briefly closed her eyes before turning away from the image of Marrakesh to walk around the rest of the large room, examining the three low couches in rich shades of burnt orange that rested in front of each wall, the brass wall sconces adding a gentle illumination to the room, the hand-painted Moorish tiles beneath their feet.

He watched her for a moment, unable to get the details of her story out of his head. Her father. His father. The cruelty of what Quentin Stanfield had done. The wrong way out that Washington Hobbes had taken. And now, years later, the repercussions of those actions reverberating between him and Diana, with the potential to shake apart their burgeoning relationship.

Marcus had always known his father had a ruthless streak, but he'd never thought he was capable of something like this. Calculated maneuvers in the boardroom were one thing, but cutting off a working man at the knees was something else altogether. All his life Marcus had worked three times as hard as his peers just to get his father's respect and to be considered even half the man he was. But if this was the man Quentin Stanfield was, what did that make of Marcus's ambitions?

Diana cleared her throat. "Thank you for showing me your home. It's large but comfortable. Trish told me you collect art. I'd imagined this massive house with a million servants and lots of museum pieces that felt very cold and boring."

"Like me?"

She looked up at him, her gaze considering, even teasing. "No. Not like you, but…" Her voice trailed off.

"Like my father, then?"

She made a face. "Yes, like your father. Even though I obviously don't know him."

"Would you like to?"

The question jumped from his lips, surprising them both. He waited for her answer.

"I… Why?"

That was a good question. Why did it matter that she got to know Quentin Stanfield? It wouldn't change what already happened between her father and his. It might even make Diana more reluctant to become involved with him.

"Never mind." He made a dismissive noise. "I should probably keep the two of you as far apart as possible."

"I think that's best. A man who can do the things he did…" She shook her head, shuddering. Diana hugged her arms and walked even farther away from him. She left her champagne glass on the floor beside his.

This wasn't exactly the mood he'd wanted to cultivate. "Come," he said. "I think we've seen everything here. Besides, there's another part of the house I want to show you."

She shot him a cool look from beneath her lashes, then took the arm he offered. They left the room, his mind touching again on his father and the things he'd done. No wonder she'd hated Marcus when she found out who his father was.

He lightly traced the bones of Diana's hand as they walked down the lushly carpeted hallway toward their next destination. He felt a faint shudder move through her, and he pulled her closer. An instinct, strong and fierce, rose suddenly in him—the instinct to cherish her and protect her. Even if it was from himself.

Chapter 17

Despite the warmth of the house, Diana felt a lingering shiver when Marcus suggested that she meet his father. Nothing on earth would convince her to meet with that man. Marcus, she knew, had nothing to do with her father's death. And her feelings for him were complicated at best. But her feelings for his father were simple. It was another matter entirely to look into the face of the man whose actions had pushed her father over the edge.

She shivered again, and Marcus gathered her against his side, warming her with the heat of his body.

"Do you want to continue with the tour?" he asked.

"Is there much more to it?"

He looked down at her from his graceful height, his gaze clearing as if he'd been thinking wholly unpleasant thoughts. "Only one more thing," he said. "But I wonder if I should hold off on that."

"Well," she said, shrugging, "we've already come this far."

A smile touched his lips as he watched her. "True."

Then he took his phone from his pocket and sent a quick text before leading her on to their next stop. As they made their way through a wide hallway, faint strains of music reached Diana. They neared a door, and Marcus stepped slightly ahead of her to open it. Johnny Hartman's rich and melodic voice floated out to greet them. She looked up at him, feeling suddenly lighter at the familiar music.

"I love Johnny Hartman," she said.

"I know." He guided her into the room with a hand at the small of her back. "I remember seeing some of his CDs in your office the night of the storm." Candlelight flickered as they walked in. "Here we are."

Diana drew a surprised breath. The room was gorgeous with its heavy, wooden furniture, high ceilings and deep burgundy walls. But what made her catch her breath was the table for two with taper candles that looked freshly lit. The table was set for a meal. Cutlery, napkins, wineglasses. All the while, Johnny Hartman sang about falling in love too easily.

"What's this?" she asked.

"Dinner." He smiled.

Marcus waved her toward the table, where he pulled out a chair for her, then settled into the seat across from her. Firelight danced on the silverware. She put her purse on the table, her head spinning from the sudden change of agenda.

"Yes, but why dinner?"

The words had barely left her mouth before a man appeared. He was dressed in formal clothes and pushed a kitchen cart. The wheels of the cart rolled over the tile and then the carpet, sending the four covered salvers rattling.

"Thank you, Ian," Marcus said.

"You're very welcome, sir."

Ian swept aside the covers of the silver trays, revealing three sumptuous meals, steam rising from them to perfume the air with their incredible aromas: fettuccine pasta with red-salmon caviar, pancetta-wrapped asparagus with a drizzle of citrus sauce and a roasted lobster split in two and sprinkled with herbs and peppers.

"Which one would you like?" Marcus looked at her expectantly.

The choices all looked delicious and beautifully plated on square white dishes.

"I'll have the asparagus," she said.

"Good choice." Marcus nodded toward the lobster for his own meal.

Ian deftly served their meals and poured white wine in their glasses before quietly withdrawing. As he wheeled the cart toward the door, Marcus called out softly, "Please see to it that we're not disturbed, Ian. And you can take the rest of the night off."

"I will, sir. Thank you." He slipped quietly outside the room and closed the door behind him.

Diana draped the cloth napkin across her lap, mimicking Marcus's relaxed posture. "So, you didn't tell me why we're having this dinner."

"Does a man need a reason to invite a beautiful woman to share a meal with him?"

"In this instance, maybe. After all, you're already hosting a party for me downstairs." Diana refused to get sidetracked by the fact that he had called her beautiful. Again. But his words still warmed her. She picked up an asparagus spear and bit into it.

"What's happening downstairs is for Building Bridges and all the children you help. This…" He gestured to the food and candles. "This is for you, the woman who has been occupying my thoughts and driving me crazy for weeks." Marcus took a sip of his wine and held her eyes with his. "I want you, but I also want to get to know you."

"Is this what you do to all the women you want? Throw money at them?"

For a moment, he looked surprised, unsettled. "I didn't realize that's what I'm doing."

"It is," she said. "Or it feels that way. This party…this party is a lot." Diana smoothed a finger along the stem of her wineglass. "I don't care about your money, Marcus."

He put down his glass and looked at her with his gold eyes darkened and serious. "I never want you to feel like I'm throwing money at you as if you mean nothing to me." But the frown came back. He pursed his lips.

"I'm just another woman in Miami. I doubt I mean very much to you."

She said the words even as she hoped they weren't true. She'd slept with him, taken shelter against a storm with him. Ever since that night, he'd eased himself into her consciousness, taking over minutes and sometimes hours of her day. He had his choice of hundreds, maybe even thousands, of women, and not simply because of his money. What could he want with a woman like Diana except another conquest?

She was falling for him despite her better judgment. Despite what her mother and brother said about him and his family. Despite his connection to Quentin Stanfield. She was torn between feeling like a traitor and wanting to follow her womanly desires.

Marcus shook his head, smiling. "You're definitely not just another woman in Miami, Diana Hobbes. From the moment I met you, I knew that."

Her face warmed. "You truly do have a silver tongue. Trish was right—you can have any woman in the world with just a few words."

He laughed. "But I don't want any woman in the world. I want you."

She flushed again and looked down at her plate. Thin pancetta twirled around the bright green asparagus spears, all topped with a drizzled yellow sauce that tasted of oranges and mustard. "Don't say things you don't mean," she said.

"I don't." Marcus took a bite of his lobster. "Look, Diana. I know things aren't ideal between us. I can't even honestly say what I want from you beyond a few days in my bed. But I do know that I want you. You're on my mind, in my thoughts in a way that no other woman has ever been." He drew a deep breath. "I'm too selfish not to pursue that."

In the background, Johnny's deep and haunting voice was mourning the loss of a romance. It felt like a premonition, but Diana felt lost in the golden gaze across from her. She wanted so much to follow after the pleasures his eyes and his smile promised. However, she had a lifetime of "buts" telling her that that was impossible.

"Marcus—"

He stood and held out a hand to her. "Dance with me."

She hesitated. Then she rose and took his hand. Diana shivered with pleasure when he drew her into his arms to the strains of a new song, Johnny singing about New York with trumpets blaring, the song both moody and mellow.

"Thank you for this," Marcus murmured into her hair.

Diana had always liked Johnny Hartman and his impossibly deep voice. Had loved him more than the better known Nat King Cole for the endless bass of his voice, the yearning in it. Tonight of all nights, his voice conveyed perfectly the sweetness she had inside her for Marcus. The pain of wanting him but also knowing that having him would hurt her family and her relationship with them.

But as he swept her around the room in his arms, with the candlelight flickering around them, the seductive trumpets pouring their music into the room, she allowed herself to be taken away, delighted and beguiled.

As she moved to the music with Marcus, a sound jarred her out of her trance. Her cell phone ringing. She looked over Marcus's shoulder to the table where she had left her leather clutch. She could practically see the small device vibrating and ringing from the confines of her purse.

It could be Jason calling. Or her sister. Or her mother. But she didn't move toward it. She only closed her eyes and immersed herself in the sounds of the music, in the feeling of Marcus's arms around her.

Before, on the night of the storm, she'd allowed herself to be taken away by the fierceness of the weather pounding outside the doors of her office building. Her heart had raced with fear from the loud thunder and lightning flashes. That fear had led her firmly into the arms of temptation. It had been a head-spinning night. Giving in to lust, to the beautiful man who made her feel at once secure and strong, desirable and unique.

That night, she had been swept away. Tonight, she had her eyes open, and she wanted to see more.

"Make love to me," she whispered.

His eyes smiled before his mouth did, taking her breath away.

She wasn't sure if she kissed him or if he kissed her. All she knew was that their lips touched and the familiar feeling took her over once again. But this time it was hotter and harder than before. She trembled in his embrace and surrendered to her desire.

Chapter 18

Marcus swept Diana into his bedroom, sharing kisses with her the whole way, her beautiful mouth opening for him, inviting tenderness and heat. The windows were open to a view of the water, the Miami cityscape across the bay, lights in the skyscrapers, stars shimmering in the sky.

He turned on the bedroom light with a trembling hand, keeping the illumination dim. She made him weak with desire. He hadn't touched or even thought of another woman since he'd met her, subconsciously saving all his passion for her. But it had been weeks since that night of the storm, days since the Carmichaels' party when she'd opened up her vulnerable heart to him and he had had the privilege of giving her pleasure. It had been a long time, and he was more than ready for her.

But tonight, she was in control. Even if she changed her mind and only kissed him good-night before heading back to the party, it would be her choice. Whatever she wanted, he would do.

Perhaps sensing her power, Diana kissed him deeply, then drew back to press her palms against his chest.

"I want to see you," she murmured.

"Whatever you want." Marcus didn't know if he said the words or just thought them, but he wasted no time giving her what she wanted; he quickly undressed.

She sighed in appreciation at his nakedness, and he felt his body prepare for her even more. "I don't think I got the chance to look at you properly before," she said.

"It was dark," he rasped as the lust pounded fiercely through him.

"And you're still beautiful." Her face was a study in wonder and desire.

She touched his bare chest, his hard belly, her fingers like silk on the dense and quivering muscles. He twitched when she went lower. Marcus held himself back from touching her, keeping his hands clenched at his sides as she explored him and saw who he was in the light.

"You're not what I expected," Diana said softly.

She took him in her hand, weighing his thickness in her palms. Marcus shuddered.

"You're a good man. You're kind and you're generous," she said. "And I want to know even more about you."

Marcus winced as his conscience twisted. He'd meant to tell her about the Baltree Heights project tonight, but each time he thought of it, something happened to derail the possible conversation. He swallowed as her hands moved on him.

Diana changed her grip, grabbed the heavy length of his sex like a rope and tugged gently. She turned then, with her hand firm but excitingly soft around him, and led him across the wide bedroom. Moonlight shone on his bare skin. The whole world watched through the open windows. Diana's bottom rocked seductively under the yellow dress as she guided him to the bed. She released him to quickly take off her clothes. Then, slowly and languorously, she unpinned her hair and allowed it to float around her face and shoulders.

Her beauty stole his breath, the confident sensuality of her as she stood basking in his admiration, hands on her hips but with something so ethereal and innocent about her at the same time. She was like no other woman in the world.

And he told her so, watching the faint color move up her throat and into her cheeks. She dipped her head for a moment, the heavy swing of hair hiding her face. Then she looked up at him again, her boldness restored. Diana sat on the edge of the bed and slowly opened her legs.

Her thighs were damp, her sex a juicy plum waiting for his mouth and his hands. Marcus trembled on the edge of implosion, knowing that if he slid into her now, he would not last long. He reached over to the bedside table for a condom and ripped open the package. He rolled the latex slowly down his long length while her eyes captured and held his.

"Marcus…"

He gave her the only answer he could. He gripped her hips, tilted her up to receive him and shoved slowly into her dripping heat. Marcus shuddered from the ecstasy of it, yearning to thrust into her again and again to reach the peak that was already so close. But he held himself back. He focused on her pleasure.

Diana's eyelashes fluttered. Her fingers clenched in the sheets. Her hips moved under his, her body clasped him, sucking him in. She was so incredible with her head thrown back, her lovely breasts bare, chest heaving with her lust. She bit her lip.

"Please!" She gasped. "Please."

Marcus moved inside her. At first he loved her deliberately, trying for slow and tender and what would make her feel best, but he quickly lost control as her breaths and her gasps filled the room. Her nails sank into his back, urging him on.

With a harsh groan, Marcus surrendered. He could only drive his hips home again and again as her wild cries filled the room like the notes of a song. Her heat gripped him and yanked him over the edge. It was humiliatingly quick.

He shuddered like a past-peak racehorse at the beginning of the race while she still writhed beneath him, searching for her satisfaction, her breath coming quickly, eyes blinking up at him in bewilderment as he stopped moving. Body still shuddering in the throes of his climax, he pulled out of her, dropped to his knees and sank his face between her thighs.

She gasped, her thighs like butterfly wings around his face, fanning wide to accommodate him. Her fingers clenched in his scalp. His tongue moved up and around the hard center of her pleasure. His name escaped from her lips. She sighed again and again, and the sun dug into his bare skin as tremors of sympathetic delight moved through him. She fell back into the bed, hips shoving up into his mouth, shuddering. And then the fluttering of her sex around his tongue as she achieved her climax. But he didn't let her go. His hands tightened on her thighs, and he sucked that delicate nub of flesh deeply in his mouth.

She bucked against his face. "Marcus!"

She was soft and wet around his fingers, sucking them deeply inside her. He curved them up, bidding her to come to him, to come for him, the slick wetness of her sex sending a tingle through his body. His desire extended beyond his shaft, beyond anything he'd ever known, overcome by

the need to please her and make her come and come and
come. Marcus stroked that delicate place inside her.

She screamed softly, then not so softly. Her fingers dug
hard in the flesh of his shoulders, then a smell of blood
rose up as she scored him, and the pain flung him hard
against her, fingers moving quickly. She burst wide open.
Just for him. Her screams of pleasure rose above his head
in a continuous wave of sound that made him go more and
harder and longer.

"Marcus!"

She snaked her sex against his face, her innermost heart
squeezing and clutching tight as she found her satisfaction again and again. He only stopped when the ache in
his knees became too much. He rose from between her
thighs to kiss her tenderly.

Diana was limp under him, her body slick with sweat,
her heart thudding like a mad thing between them. "I don't
think I could even walk right now," she breathed.

"Good." He chuckled and pressed a kiss to her throat.
"The last thing I want is for you to walk away from me."

In the aftermath of their lovemaking, Marcus lay in
bed with Diana resting her head against his chest. She
breathed softly against him, misting his skin. He felt absolutely boneless with satisfaction, his body and soul truly
content for the first time in a very long while. Maybe ever.

Diana's fingers stirred on his chest a moment before she
sat up and stretched. Her gaze moved slowly over his body,
an indolent and thorough journey that made his muscles
twitch and his sex begin to thicken against his thigh. He
braced his hands against the bed, palms down, allowing
her to look her fill.

The white sheets were like silk under his bare skin as
her gaze stroked him to further hardness. Desire for her

pooled in his middle, spreading out to every part of him. He curled his fingers in the sheets to stop himself from reaching for her. He tipped his head back into the pillows instead, released a soft breath and watched the plump softness of her lips.

"You look like you were born to this life," she murmured, her hand only a few inches from his thigh. "Luxury suits you."

"Looks can be deceiving." He returned her gaze.

"I doubt that very much," she said. "And I like your looks."

He thought he detected a faint hint of color under her cheeks at that admission. "You're an open book," she said. "I like that about you. Rich playboy about town. Born into money. Happy to spend it. Good at making more of it."

He felt that familiar mixture of pleasure and chagrin whenever someone mentioned him being born into the Stanfield family. He opened his mouth to offer the usual pithy and offhand remark about his family and certain things being learned not inherited. But...

"I was actually adopted," he said.

She tilted her head down toward him, as if she didn't quite trust her ears. "What?"

"I wasn't born into this life," he said. "I was accepted into it. Quentin Stanfield adopted me when I was four years old. He and his wife at the time were unable to have children, so they found me and took me home with them." He said the words, grateful at how casual they sounded. It had taken him years to say them without a half apology that he wasn't quite who the listener thought he was. To tell them he was worth the Stanfield name and worked twice as hard to make his father proud of the man he'd become. Proud that he had not made a mistake in taking Marcus in.

Diana blinked, her lips parting in surprise. "I had no idea."

"Although it's a matter of public record, not many people seem to know about it," he said. "Or maybe they just don't mention it out of politeness." He shrugged, watching her face to see her reaction.

Would she pull away? Find him no longer worthy? He'd wrestled with those questions so often they'd become automatic when someone found out about his adoption.

"Oh, wow…" She tilted her head, smiling. "That's a beautiful surprise," she said.

"Is it?"

"Of course." Her smile widened, showing teeth, the tiny lines at the corners of her eyes and mouth. She came close to him again, lay her head on his chest. "It means you're even more complicated than I thought."

He laughed softly, gathering her even closer to him.

"Don't mistake previous orphanhood for depth, lovely Diana. The only thing that being the Stanfield chosen child has done is make me grateful for the life I have." He threaded his fingers through her thick hair. "Sometimes I wonder what would have happened to me if I had never been adopted." A lump formed in his throat as he vocalized the thought for the first time.

"There's no need for you to wonder about that," she said. "Your life happened the way it did, and that's enough. All you can do is help make a better life for others when you can, which I know you do."

How would she know anything about that? The angelic woman wanted to make him seem like one of her kind.

"Don't try to make me a saint just because I wasn't born into money, angel."

She vibrated with gentle laughter against him. "I wouldn't be misguided enough to think of you as a saint,

Marcus Stanfield." She stressed his last name with a twist of her lips.

"Touché."

She laughed again, her fingers moving lightly over his chest. The feel of her delicate hand on him brought arousal trickling into Marcus's belly.

He rolled over, reversing their positions in the bed. His hips pressed into hers, and he swallowed at the thick sensation that moved through him. Diana made an incoherent sound, her nails digging into his biceps. He smoothed strands of hair from her face, admiring the way the fine brown skin looked under the room's dim lights. Marcus kissed her cheek, her throat.

"I know we need to get back to the party but…"

"Oh, my God! The party!" She blinked quickly, eyes clearing as if waking from a dream. Her soft hands pressed against his chest. "We have to get back."

That was the last thing he wanted to do, but he released a sigh of regret and kissed her mouth once more.

"All right," he said. "Let's go."

Marcus showed her to the bathroom, where she quickly showered and got dressed. While she fiddled with her hair and makeup, he took a fast shower of his own. Within twenty minutes, they were both dressed and walking down the stairs toward the party.

But, heading back into the thick of the event he had planned just for her, Marcus couldn't help but linger on what they had just shared. The rawness and beauty of their bodies coming together—and the truth of his adoption that had come spilling out of him so unexpectedly. He not only wanted her, he also trusted her.

Nothing about his involvement with Diana Hobbes had

gone as planned. Nothing. He was both excited and apprehensive about what else was to come. Whatever it was, he hoped that neither of them would regret it.

Chapter 19

Leaving Marcus's bedroom was like traveling from one world to another. Diana walked at her lover's side, unable to believe it had only been an hour or two since they'd left the party. The music sounded the same, the people laughing and networking and spending their money all seemed unchanged, but inside she felt...renewed.

Marcus had been a passionate and attentive lover, giving her what she needed again and again, kissing her, telling her how beautiful she was to him while he lifted her body to even greater heights than before. The candlelight, his tenderness, the thoughts he'd shared with her in his bed—all these things made her see him in a new light, made her glad to surrender her suspicion of him and the last of her reluctance to become involved with Quentin Stanfield's son.

She and Marcus stepped into the vast ballroom where the band played a remix of one of Alice Smith's songs.

"Marcus, what's good?"

A slender man emerged from the crowd, dapper in a crisp white dinner jacket with a red handkerchief in the pocket and wearing a pair of tight jeans that showed off muscled thighs and narrow hips. His looks were a watered-down version of Tyson Beckford, not as chiseled but decent enough.

"Garrick." Marcus greeted the man with a cool nod, his hand at the small of Diana's back as he prepared to escort her across the room to where Nora stood talking with an older man. "Good to see you," Marcus said to the man, although he clearly didn't mean it.

Garrick shook Marcus's hand, but his gaze immediately turned to Diana. She felt his sudden interest like a physical touch.

"Oh, man." He glanced between Marcus and Diana. "She's not your usual style at all, but she's a hot piece. You want to share her later?"

Marcus stopped dead in the center of the room. "What did you say?" His voice was a shard of glass.

Diana stiffened. "You could never get that lucky," she said coldly.

Marcus's hand snapped out and gripped Garrick's wrist, pressing his hand up and backward. "Apologize to the lady." His voice was low and dangerous, growling from behind his clenched teeth. "That was uncalled for."

The man winced in pain, easing forward to try to lessen the agony of Marcus's grip. "Damn, take it easy! It's not like you haven't shared your castoffs before." At Marcus's growl, he made another noise. "Sorry, damn! I didn't mean anything by it."

Marcus dropped the man's hand as if it were filth, wiped his palm on his thigh and escorted Diana away.

She could feel the fury in the stiff line of his body. They

made their way slowly across the room in silence. Just before they reached Nora, he stopped and pulled her aside.

"I'm sorry about that." He took a deep, trembling breath. "That shouldn't have happened. I'm sorry you had to deal with it."

"It's fine. I deal with worse jerks during my work week." But the things the man had hinted at, that Marcus passed his women on to other men like cars or discarded clothes, alarmed her.

Marcus shook his head. "Don't—" He drew another breath, a deeper one that hinted at something he did not want to say. "You're important to me. You mean... I'll never expose you to something like that again." He touched her waist. "Please believe me."

Diana bit the inside of her lip. "I don't know—"

"Marcus, I wondered where you'd gone off to."

Diana looked up at the sound of another male voice. She stiffened, prepared for another verbal assault by a Miami pretty boy, but when she looked up, anything that she had planned to say got stuck in her throat.

"Dad." Marcus greeted the man who walked across the crowded room toward them. "I didn't know you were coming tonight." A frown creased his brow as he looked apologetically at Diana.

"Is it all right that I'm here to support my son?" Quentin Stanfield grinned wolfishly as he gripped his son's hand in a firm handshake and briefly squeezed his shoulder. He turned to Diana.

"Who is this lovely young lady?"

Marcus froze for a moment before he visibly gathered himself. "Dad, this is Diana Hobbes." He turned to her. "Diana, this is my father, Quentin Stanfield."

She felt encased in ice, not knowing what to say or do as the man she had hated from afar for so long took her hand in his and pressed his lips to the back of her knuckles. *"Enchantée, madame."*

Wearing a hand-tailored pinstriped suit with a paisley tie, he appeared even more powerful in the flesh. The newspaper photos had been flattering but barely showed the strength in his broad shoulders, the fierce glint to the eyes that flashed around the room, completely taking in his surroundings.

Diana clenched her teeth and firmly pulled her hand back. "Mr. Stanfield."

He seemed oblivious to her coolness, however, as he turned back to his son. "Pardon me for interrupting," he said. "I didn't feel like being at home tonight. Aliza is doing the jealous second-wife thing again and breaking all the dishes in the pantry. I can't deal with that right now." He looked around the room. "The women here seem sane enough. I just might enjoy one of them for company tonight."

Diana looked at Marcus, who didn't seem at all shocked by his father's planned infidelity and the casual way he spoke for anyone to hear.

"You're welcome to stay as long as you like, Dad. Just like everyone else." He smiled slightly. "Just don't break any of my dishes while you're here."

"Excuse me, Mr. Stanfield." Diana finally broke through the ice around her throat. "Do you remember my father, Washington Hobbes?" She felt the eyes of both Stanfield men on her.

Quentin Stanfield frowned, shoving his hands in his pants pockets. "No, I don't. Should I?"

"He used to work in one of your factories. It was many years ago."

He shook his head. "Then I wouldn't remember him."

"You should remember his name. You killed him."

Diana felt her voice rising the more she talked. "You stole his pension, and he killed himself not long after because he couldn't support his family anymore."

Quentin Stanfield drew in a swift breath, his chest expanding even more. "You are a very presumptuous young woman."

"My father didn't raise me to wait until I was acknowledged," she said coolly.

"According to what you just said, he didn't raise you at all."

Diana gasped, surprised at how much his words hurt. She clenched her fists at her side. "You ba—"

"Dad." Marcus had a hint of steel in his voice.

Quentin Stanfield ignored his son. "I don't remember anything about your father and his life, Ms. Hobbes, but I can assure you what happened was just business and nothing at all personal. I made my choices and so did your father." Then he turned to Marcus. "Is this the kind of woman you're running around with these days, son?"

Diana felt a few gazes turn to the three of them as Quentin Stanfield raised his voice. But most people quickly averted their eyes and pretended to be absorbed in other things. It may have been her imagination, but the music seemed to play a little louder, get more cheerful.

"Yes, I am seeing her these days. She is also a strong woman who I respect," Marcus said. "I don't appreciate your tone of voice when you're speaking to her."

Diana frowned when she saw a hint of admiration in Quentin Stanfield's face, a flash of pride. The elder Stanfield looked at her. "It was interesting meeting you, young lady. Perhaps I'll see you again." He glanced at his son. "Let's talk on Monday." Then he touched Marcus's shoulder briefly before disappearing into the crowd.

Marcus cursed softly. "I'm sorry about that." He put his arms around her, holding her close.

Diana looked through the crowd where the older man had gone, feeling her stomach slowly unclench. Quentin Stanfield was truly unrepentant. A hard man who seemed to have little conscience. But meeting and talking with him had brought an odd sort of relief—not only in being able to confront the man who had affected her family's life so strongly, but also to see how unlike him Marcus was. She released a long breath as she leaned into her lover's chest.

"It's okay," she said. "I'm okay."

The rest of the night was a blur of networking in the name of Building Bridges. Diana barely had time to think about the encounter with Marcus's father and what it meant. She held it all at bay until Nora gave her a big hug, grateful to tears for the final total of nearly four hundred thousand dollars that the party managed to raise.

When she looked at her phone at the end of the night, she saw that she had missed two calls from her brother and nearly a dozen text messages from Trish. Her best friend had been in a playful mood, asking in increasingly explicit terms if Diana had managed to sleep with Marcus again. She ignored the X-rated messages and decided to call her brother back the next morning, especially after she listened to his voice mail and found out he only wanted to borrow her car again.

Finally, it was after one in the morning. The last members of the band were walking out the door with their instruments. The house was quiet, most of the lights had been turned down, and the staff had gone to their beds.

Marcus sat at the bottom of the stairs with his shirt sleeves rolled up to his elbows and his jacket discarded on the steps by his side. He looked beguiling, sexy with his heavy-lidded gold eyes watching her walk tiredly across the ballroom toward him.

"Thank you for staying until the end," he said.

"Thank you for having this party." Her heels sounded hollowly against the marble floor as she crossed the empty room.

Marcus held out a hand, palm up. "You should spend the night with me," he said. "Spend the weekend." He smiled crookedly.

She put her hand in his, and he pulled her down into his lap. His warm skin held a hint of sandalwood cologne.

"I can't," she said, although she was tempted. Diana draped her arm over his shoulder and settled into his hard furnace of a body.

The hour in his bed had given her just a preview of how things could be with him. Passion and tenderness, evening confessions and safe arms to hold her while she slept. Someone to trust.

"Why?" he asked. "Why can't you be with me? What would you be running back home to?" He trailed light fingers up her bare arm, sending tingles running through her body. "Do you have another man waiting for you? A family I don't know about? A bunch of little kids?"

She shook her head, smiling. "No. None of those things."

"Then stay."

And so she did.

Chapter 20

Diana was the happiest she'd ever been. Functioning on little sleep, she drove home from Marcus's place with just enough time to get dressed for work and make her breakfast smoothie. She sang softly to herself in the kitchen, her blender growling into the otherwise quiet morning. Her hand drifted to touch her neck as thoughts of Marcus and the days they had spent wrapped in each other took her over.

The weekend with Marcus had been more than she'd ever dreamed. Hours spent indulging in intimate touches, in conversation, laying herself bare to another human being in a way she'd never done before. Marcus had teased her, fed her, loved her so well that she had been reluctant to leave his house and the addictive kisses he gave with as much frequency as she liked. It had been magical.

Even showered and dressed in her day armor of high heels, gray jersey dress and a fall of bright malachite stones around her throat, she felt him. She heard him. The sounds of his deep moans, the filthy things he breathed in her ear as they loved. Diana trembled. Fumbled to turn off the blender before the machine burned itself out. She pressed her thighs together as she unscrewed the blender attachment, then rinsed it under a gush of cool water before dropping it into the top rack of the dishwasher.

Marcus.

Marcus.

Marcus.

She trembled but tried to pull herself together.

Diana looked at her watch. 8:15. She grabbed her smoothie, then her briefcase and purse that were waiting by the door and stepped outside her house, keys jingling in her hand.

She stopped short at the sight of her brother's car in the driveway. Jason was sitting on her porch swing, a belligerent look on his face. She frowned as she locked the door. "What are you doing here, Jason?"

"You never returned any of my calls. I know you were with *him*." He said "him" like he was talking about the devil.

Diana fought a flash of defensiveness, annoyed that he was trying to bring down her buoyant morning. "What do you want?"

Her brother stood up from the swing, sending the bench clanging on its chains. "He screwed you all weekend, and now he's going to screw you even harder later this week," Jason said.

A hot tide of embarrassment moved under her skin. "I told you what I do with Marcus is none of your business."

"Do you even understand what I'm telling you?"

"If you think I don't, why don't you make yourself clearer so I can get to work? I don't want to be late."

"Your boyfriend is buying up all of Baltree Heights.

Soon you won't have a job to walk to. He's going to tear down everything on that street to build a condo or some crappy parking garage."

Diana almost choked on her breath. "What are you talking about?"

Her brother looked impatient with her stupidity. "Marcus Stanfield just bought up all the land in Baltree Heights. He's not planning on being a landlord to a bunch of people who already pay cheap rent. He's going to tear everything down and build something that makes him more money."

"How do you even know that?" She frowned. Her brother would do anything to get Marcus out of her life. "I didn't know marine-biology students have the ear of real-estate developers in Miami."

His jaw twitched in anger. "Trish told me."

"Trish?"

"Yeah. I asked her to check into him for me while you were gone."

Diana frowned. "Why didn't she tell me that?"

Jason crossed his arms over his chest in defiance. "If you don't believe me, just ask Marcus Stanfield. If he's not a liar, he'll tell you what I said is the truth."

"I can't deal with this now, Jason," she said tiredly. "Just leave this alone. Marcus is in my life. It's time that you and Mom got over that."

He made a sound of disgust. "I hope it's worth it for you to betray your family like this. The cost of a few nights in his bed."

She wanted to slap him. Instead, she clenched her hands into fists and turned away, her shoes stabbing into the pavement with each step. Jason was the youngest of the Hobbes children, but the older he became, the more he acted like the parent, simply because he was the only man in the family. She was sick of it.

But as she walked to the office, his words haunted her. Why would her brother say something like that if it wasn't true? But would Marcus be so heartless? Building Bridges had become such an important part of her life. Seeing the children they helped being placed in loving homes filled her with so much joy and purpose.

Through her work with Building Bridges, the dissatisfactions from the years without a lover in her bed, of not being able to travel because of work or her obligations to family, had begun to dwindle. There was no way the man Marcus had shown himself to be over the weekend would compromise that. No way.

At Building Bridges, she climbed up the steps onto the porch. It was as if the hurricane had never been. Before their landlord had even gotten the chance to respond, an anonymous donor had sent over workmen and repaired everything during the course of a weekend.

At 9:02, by her watch, she opened the front door to the house and stepped inside. The slow murmurings of a Monday morning greeted her, along with the smell of coffee in the air.

"Good morning, Carla."

Diana paused at the receptionist's desk to greet the young girl. Almost completely hiding Carla's face was a bright bouquet of flowers. Lush purple irises. Pink blushed white lilies. Yellow roses.

They smelled sweet. Something about the combination of scents reminded her suddenly of Marcus's bedroom. A flutter moved through her stomach at the thought of him, a pleasant counterpoint to the worry she'd tortured herself with on the walk to work.

"Good morning, Diana." The receptionist gave a wide smile, even wider than usual. "These came for you a few minutes ago."

Diana smiled with pleasure as the girl pointed to the flowers.

"There's even a card." Carla passed the card to Diana, who immediately put it in her dress pocket. She didn't have to look to see who'd sent the flowers. "Thank you."

Still smiling, she didn't give in to the girl's obvious curiosity, only grabbed the heavy vase and walked on through to her office.

"Nice buds!" Willa, their accountant, remarked as Diana passed down the narrow aisle of desks toward her office. Her brown face was still creased with a smile.

"Somebody had a great weekend!" Nora came around the corner, an iPad and her purse in her hands. She glanced at the flowers with a smile. "Did you even make it home after the fund-raiser?"

Diana couldn't stop the wide grin that tripped across her face. Then she reigned it in at Nora's look of surprise. "That's for me to know and you to never find out," she tossed over her shoulder as she walked into her office. She carefully placed the flowers on her desk and put aside her things before sinking into her chair to open the card.

Diana.
Thank you for a weekend I'll never forget.
I want to do this again with you soon.
Yours, Marcus.

Diana bit her lip, tugging back the smile that threatened to run away from her. She looked up at the sound of footsteps. Willa stood in the doorway.

"A hot date this weekend?"

Diana wondered how much she should say. She'd never had anything personal to share at the office before. Then she mentally shrugged. "Yes, actually."

"Good. It's about time. I'm happy for you."

Color surged under her skin. It was a well-known secret in the office that she didn't have much of a life outside of Building Bridges and her family, and it had never bothered Diana before. But something about the other woman's words made her flush with something like embarrassment. She never minded being the workaholic before. Never minded being the woman who was always at the office before everyone else and the last to leave. The work fulfilled her, gave her everything she needed to be happy.

But now, seeing the look on Willa's face, remembering the pleased expression Carla wore, she realized how much they must have thought her life was lacking. How much, perhaps, it had been.

But she didn't want her life's changes, what there were of them, to simply be because of Marcus Stanfield. Talking with her brother that morning had rankled her more than she liked to admit. It made her doubt Marcus. Made her doubt what she was feeling.

"Willa." She tapped a finger against her thigh under the desk as she gave second thoughts to what she was about to say. "Have you heard anything about developers buying up the land around here?"

"No, I haven't. But if something's happening, Nora would know." She shrugged, then offered a folder to Diana. "Here is the file for the Williamsons. Their security check and financials came back clean. They're a go to adopt little Felix."

Diana shrugged aside her personal concerns as she slid Marcus's card into the top drawer of her desk and opened the manila folder. "Okay, great. I'll have Melissa call the agency today to let them know, then we can begin paying the necessary fees to get that little boy into his new home."

"Great! I have a few more on my desk that should be

done by the end of the day." Willa turned to leave. "Oh, by the way, you did know that the Sorensons were denied, right?"

Diana paused with the folder between her fingers, frowning. "Yes. Our security firm saw some signs that they might be linked to a child sex ring. He contacted Vic over at Miami-Dade Police about them."

"That's a damn shame. It just goes to show you never know the true character of the person smiling in your face. That smiling face is not always the real one."

Once Willa was gone, she forced herself to turn to the task at hand and away from thoughts of Marcus. She turned on her computer and began her tasks for the day.

Once she finished up her morning list, she went to find Nora in her office. She walked in carefully, waiting until her boss got off the phone before asking her the same question she'd asked Willa earlier that morning.

"Have you heard anything about investors buying up property around here?"

The chair squeaked as Nora leaned back. "I heard a few things through the board at my condo. You know I don't live too far from here." Nora made a vague gesture north. "I was a little worried but didn't want to invest too much energy into the rumor in case it isn't true." Her boss tapped a pen against her neatly arranged desk. "But in the past week or so, we've received a few large donations that will cover the cost of our relocation. If it should come down to that."

Diana frowned. "Large? How large?" *And why didn't you tell me?*

"Over a million dollars."

Diana blinked in surprise.

"That's not even including the money from the fund-raiser on Friday night."

Diana was shocked by the sheer amount of money. The cost of what they did for the children and their prospective families wasn't cheap—security checks, adoption fees, helping them to get their homes ready for the arrival of a child. Building Bridges had been getting by with steady donations from reliable donors as well as from their annual fund-raisers. But they'd never raised so much money at one time. Suspicion gnawed at her. Was Marcus paying to make his guilt go away?

"That's great that we have so much now," she said, dazed by the thoughts swirling through her head. "Really great."

Suddenly, she needed to talk with Marcus. "Thanks for chatting with me about this," she said. "I'm going on an errand, but I'll be back for our meeting later this afternoon."

Nora didn't bat an eye. She knew Diana would more than make up for any time she took off. "Okay. See you at the meeting." She tipped her head in Diana's direction and turned back to the phone.

Diana left her boss's office, grabbed her purse and walked home. She wasn't quite sure where she was going at first. To Marcus's house? To Trish's? To her favorite coffee shop to fret more about the situation?

In the end, she found herself at Marcus's place. At the gate, the guard called Marcus, who gave permission for her to drive up to the house. He was out back on his boat, apparently.

It was barely eleven in the morning, and the air smelled clean and fresh, as if all the filth had been washed away, leaving the world a place where nothing could go wrong. Where everything was right and people did things out of love. It was a naive enough feeling that Diana released her breath with each second that passed.

She parked her car in front of the massive house and took the long walk from the circular drive down the cement path, through a manicured garden and out to the back of the mansion. The exterior was as beautiful as the interior. It was an impressive Spanish style, with the many terraces overlooking the turquoise pool and the bay where Marcus's boat floated on the water. Sunlight reflected up in a torrid sparkle on the underside of the boat, the *Dirty Diana*. Water slapped against the white hull in a soothing rhythm.

Diana was staring up at the boat, wondering if she had the courage to board it and confront Marcus when she heard the light sound of footsteps. He appeared on the deck, carefree and handsome in shorts that were loose around his narrow hips and flapped around his knees. His bare chest glistened in the sun.

"Diana! What a surprise."

He jogged across the deck and climbed quickly from the boat, his smile eager and unrestrained. "Did you get my flowers?"

Marcus was so beautiful. It was all she could do not to throw herself into his arms. Diana took a few careful steps back. "Are you buying up the land in Baltree Heights?"

He stopped short. The smile dropped from his face like a lead balloon. His look said it all.

She sucked in a breath, surprised by how much it hurt. "Marcus…" His name left her mouth in a hoarse whisper. She blinked from the sudden tears, her fist tight against her belly. "How could you do that?"

The muscle clenched in his jaw. "The plan was set in motion long before I met you," he said.

"Does it matter? You're displacing dozens of people. You're ruining the community."

"Nothing is ruined, Diana. It's business. Everyone who owned property will be well-compensated for their land. You know that."

"But what about Building Bridges? What about the people in the neighborhood who can't afford to go anywhere else? What about the people whose taxes are going up once you come in and rip apart the community?" She bit her lip before she could say anymore. "I thought you were better than that."

"It's not the end of the world, Diana. I'm sure we can work something out for Building Bridges."

"Like the money you helped us raise? Nearly half a million dollars, Marcus? Is that how much it cost to appease your conscience?"

"This is not about my conscience. It's about taking care of the nonprofit so it can find a new home without an interruption in its business." He paused. "Nora doesn't see anything wrong with it."

"Nora?" She made a dismissive sound. "She's too naive to know any better." Diana shook her head, unable to believe he was so cavalier about what he was doing to both the nonprofit and to the neighborhood. He of all people should know the importance of investing in black communities so they could thrive instead of being gobbled up and forced out like so many others across the country.

He moved toward her, a hand stretched out. "Diana, please see my perspective—"

She flinched from him. "I just can't believe you'd be so selfish when you could have bought land in any other part of the city. Make your millions some other way aside from at the expense of the people in Baltree Heights. Your people."

"Don't bring race into this conversation."

"It never left the conversation." She clenched her teeth and stepped back from him. "I can't look at you right now. I just can't." Her chin wobbled with the onset of tears, but she steadied it. "You're not the man I thought you were." She turned to walk away.

But he grabbed her arm. "I am that man. The actions of this deal do not reflect who I am." His hand was hot around her upper arm. "I'm a good man, Diana. I'm the man for you."

She jerked her arm away from him, or she at least tried to. "No, Marcus. You're neither of those things. You're just as opportunistic and heartless as your father. Worse. At least he never led anyone to believe he is anything other than what he is."

He released her suddenly, his face abruptly shuttered. The look almost made her take back what she said. Almost. She was so accustomed to his open look. Laughter. Desire. Tenderness. Not this blank page she couldn't read. She felt herself weakening.

No. It wasn't just about her and Marcus. Not only had he betrayed her, but he also had betrayed her community and the work she was doing.

Diana left him there. She left the dock and the boat that bore her name and the man whose face she no longer recognized. In her car, the tears flowed freely, running down her face in a blinding stream. Her fingernails dug into the steering wheel as she forced herself to navigate the car down the long drive and through the high steel gates. She had trusted him. Opened herself up to him, and all the while he had been planning this?

Her mother was right. Her brother was right. Marcus was no better than his father. She drove away from the mansion weighed down by the most sadness she'd carried in a long time. The betrayal cut more deeply than she ever thought possible. Trapped in a well of grief, Diana drove to her house, parked the car in her garage and turned off the engine. She sat there in the dark for a long while, not knowing what else to do.

Chapter 21

Diana didn't know how she was able to go back to work, but she did. She finished the work day, even stayed late, clearing her mind of everything but what she needed to do her job. She didn't talk to Nora about the sale of the land and their building. She figured her boss would find out about it soon enough and take the necessary steps. Diana's main concern was making sure that none of their plans and cases got interrupted or derailed because of the move.

At nearly eight o'clock, she left the office and went home. She walked into her darkened house, wanting to talk to somebody. Anybody. The conversation she'd had with Marcus still weighed heavily on her. Beyond her capacity to carry alone.

She called Trish.

"What's wrong?" Trish asked the question before Diana could get past "Hello."

Diana bit her trembling lip as she sat down on the bed. "It—"

"Don't say it's nothing. I can tell you have something going on from all the way over here." The sound of rustling came through the phone. Trish in her own bed across town. "Do you want me to come over there?"

"No, no." She pressed her lips together.

"Is it about Marcus Stanfield?"

There was no use denying it. "Yes."

"What did he do?"

Haltingly, the words came from her lips. Their hookup at the dinner party. Their easy passion. The betrayal.

"The whole time he was romancing me, he was planning to destroy Building Bridges!" she sobbed.

Trish let her cry for a moment. Then she sighed softly through the phone. "Don't you think you're being a little dramatic about that, Diana? It's just business. And all this started before you two got together."

"Why do you always take his side?" Diana sniffed and wiped away the tears with the back of her hand.

"It's not his side, honey," Trish said. "I'm on the side of whatever makes you happy. If—"

The sound of another call coming through interrupted her friend's voice. Diana looked down at the phone. It was Marcus. Her breath caught.

"What is it?"

Diana stuttered, then tried again until his name came out of her mouth. "It's Marcus on the other line."

"Answer it!"

"No!"

"Yes. See if he has anything different to say."

They argued fiercely back and forth while the tone rang insistently in Diana's ear.

"Go answer it, or I'm going to call him back myself," Trish finally said.

Diana clicked over. "Hello."

It was nothing but dead air for a moment. Silence. Then the sound of breath. His voice. Her stomach clenched hard. Her heartbeat was deafening in her ears.

"Diana. I killed the deal." Another breath. "I don't want this to come between us. I know you don't understand my point of view, but I see yours. I understand."

Her tight grip on the phone loosened as the lump tightened in her throat. "Okay. Thanks."

Silence again. His breath. Her breath.

"I'll talk with you another time," she said, then hung up the phone without waiting for his response. She went back to the call with Trish.

"What did he say?"

"That the deal is off. He won't buy in Baltree Heights anymore."

Trish made a noise of triumph. "See? I told you he was a good guy."

Diana twisted and untwisted the hem of her nightgown between her fingers. It was more than that. It hurt her deeply that he had been willing to go through with it despite knowing how much Building Bridges meant to her. The betrayal ran deeply through her. But even she had to admit his leaving Baltree Heights alone went a long way toward fixing things between them.

"I can't believe he was willing to do that, Trish."

"Honey, he may give money to charity, but he's still a businessman. I've dated men who had their eye on Baltree Heights. If Marcus doesn't snap it up, it's only a matter of time before someone else does." Trish's breath blew against the phone. "He must be throwing away millions of dollars because of you."

"Not because of me. Because he's doing the right thing."

Trish sighed again. "Sometimes I wonder at how naive you are, honey."

"What are you talking about?"

"The world does not run on sunshine and flowers. To be able to do the things you do, someone has to get down in the muck and deal with the filth of life."

"But he's not doing that—he's selling our neighborhoods!"

"Enough of this pointless debate," Trish said with exasperation in her voice. "Let's go out for a drink. You can give me all the details of Marcus's stroking technique in person."

Diana drew a swift breath. "Trish!"

"What?" Trish asked. "It's not like I'm asking you for a show-and-tell."

Chapter 22

Marcus disconnected the call with Diana and sank back in his chair, putting his cell phone on the table. On the other side of the boat, Seven was stretched out on one of the leather benches, ankles crossed, a whiskey sour in his hand. The ocean lapped against the hull, the sound reaching Marcus through the open portholes.

"Did you lose that woman with your typical foolishness?" Seven asked. His wedding ring clinked against the glass as he sipped his drink.

"Not the typical kind," Marcus said, cursing himself for the hundredth time since Diana came to see him.

"At least she picked up your call," Seven said.

"Yeah…I was worried for a minute that she wouldn't." Marcus couldn't stop the twinge of anxiety that clenched his jaw.

"Did you really stop the deal?" Seven raised an eyebrow in his direction.

"Of course. I wouldn't lie to her."

"Only by omission," Seven said with a wry twist of his mouth.

Even knowing what his friend said was the truth, Marcus made an irritated noise. He tapped his fingers against the table, wincing at the memory of Diana's visit that morning.

He had meant to tell her, but the timing had never seemed to be right. But it had been stupid of him to push the deal through in the first place once he found out that her nonprofit was part of it. His father had been furious when Marcus told him he wanted to cancel Baltree and even more so when Marcus shared with him the reason. Despite the intense disappointment in his father's eyes, he had stuck to his guns. It hadn't been easy. But he'd done it.

The change of heart meant a significant financial loss to him. But it was money he could easily make back some other way. If he was going to be completely honest with himself, he'd have to admit that he had gone through with the deal in the first place to please his father.

Quentin Stanfield had wanted to get into the gentrification business. He wanted to start with the property smack-dab in the middle of Baltree Heights. Knowing this, Marcus called his father in on the deal, planned on giving him the property to seal them working together for the first time since he loaned Marcus the two million dollars to invest in a budding project more than ten years before.

He had long ago paid the two million back—with interest his father had at first refused—but he never forgot Quentin Stanfield's generosity. And he never forgot how his father had brought him into the family, had chosen Marcus over so many others. Had still loved him even after the Stanfields had been able to conceive their own children.

The sound of a glass tapping gently against the wooden

table brought him back to himself. Seven had finished his drink and was watching him with an amused look.

"You're whipped bad," his friend said.

Marcus shook his head, about to deny it. But he couldn't. And it was more than just the sex. More than the fact of her divine beauty that stirred both his protective urge and his baser ones. "I want her to forgive me," he said.

"I think you'll have to do a bit more than stop being a prick." Seven stood up. "It's been fun, but I'm heading back home to Bailey. We have dinner plans."

"Speaking of being whipped..." Marcus chuckled weakly.

It was moments like this when he almost envied what Seven and Bailey had found together. A love that seemed liberating rather than restraining, no matter how much he teased his friend about running back home to his wife.

"Later, man." Seven stretched his lanky frame and headed for the stairs that would take him up on deck.

"Yeah," Marcus said with a brief nod. "Give Bailey my best."

He stared off into space as his friend's footsteps faded away, wondering if Diana would forgive him—wondering if he even deserved to be forgiven.

Chapter 23

Diana grabbed her keys on her way out the door. She'd had a long day at work, where she'd fielded questions about her and Marcus, about why she looked so normal when only days before she'd been practically glowing. The answer was Marcus, and it seemed like it always would be.

After drinks a few nights before with Trish, she felt a little better. But the betrayal still stung her heart. She felt that all her trust had been misplaced. Then there was the imminent displacement of Building Bridges. It made her angry every time she thought about it. Keys in hand, Diana shoved open the door, then gasped at the sight of the slight form stepping onto her porch. Silver hair. A face neatly lined from years of emotional pain and worry.

"Mother?"

"Diana."

Her mother stood on the porch in a floral blouse and black capri pants. Her big white Cadillac was parked in the driveway.

Diana stared at her in shock. Cheryl Hobbes-Freeman never left her house for anything other than shopping and errands. "What are you doing here?"

"You didn't think I'd hear about you and Marcus Stanfield and stay away, did you?" Her mother's face was a study in coolness. Today she seemed fully in control of her emotions as she turned the full weight of her stare onto Diana. It had been more than a month since they'd seen each other at one of their rare Sunday dinners at her mother's house. That had been less than a week before she met Marcus.

Diana turned away from her mother, fully intending to lock her front door and talk with her mother on the porch.

"Don't turn your back on me, Diana Hobbes! What you've already done is unforgivable. Don't add this to it."

"Mother, please." She already felt like she'd been crushed into the pit of the earth because of what happened with Marcus. The love she thought she'd found with him. The connection and rapport she thought they shared. All gone.

"Invite me in," her mother commanded.

Diana sighed softly before opening the door and pushing it wide for her mother to follow her inside. She dropped the keys into the glass bowl by the door. In the kitchen, she poured two glasses of fresh-squeezed pineapple juice.

She didn't want to talk about Marcus. She didn't want to relive any of what happened between them. But she knew that her mother had something heavy on her mind, something she was going to say, whether or not Diana wanted to hear it.

She brought the drinks into the living room and put one in front of her mother, who was already sitting on the couch with her purse beside her. Diana sat across from her in the armchair, clasping her hands in her lap. Her usual attitude was to wait when it was obvious her mother had something to say. She didn't have to wait long.

"I'm so disappointed in you, Diana."

She swallowed, clenching her hands in her lap as her mother continued.

"You let that man touch you. You let him turn you away from your family."

"He didn't turn me away from anything, Mother," Diana said, refusing to keep silent at that. "I'm still here."

"No, you're not. Your brother called on the weekend you spent with Marcus Stanfield. Jason could have been dead in the gutter for all you knew." Her mother frowned, leaning toward Diana. "He could have really needed you."

She blushed, remembering where she was when her brother called. "I checked my voice mail. Jason was fine. He's fine now. He just hates Marcus for what his father did, nothing else."

Her mother's eyes narrowed. "You know that's not true. Jason told me he's buying up everything near your adoption house, that place you work." She gripped her purse, a satisfied look on her face as if glad all she'd predicted was coming true. "He's going to buy all those buildings and rip your office and everything you've worked for to the ground."

"He won't." She felt like a child protesting the existence of darkness simply because she didn't want it to be in her world. "He's not going to buy Baltree Heights anymore. He changed his mind."

"If you believe that, then you're more of a fool than your father ever was."

Diana drew in a breath of surprised pain. For a moment, she couldn't speak. She could only stare at her mother with tears blurring the edges of her sight. Her father was a fool?

And now she was a fool, too? Diana shook her head and stood up from the chair.

"Mother, I think you should go."

Her mother leaned back in the couch, watching Diana. Slowly, her face softened into something resembling tenderness. "Baby, I only say these things to make you realize that you have to be stronger."

Diana crossed her arms over her chest. She bit the inside of her cheek, pushing aside the tears that threatened. "I've been strong for this whole family since I was sixteen years old," she said. "When will the family ever be strong for me?" Tears slipped down her cheeks, salting her tongue. "I love him. God help me, I do. I may be stupid for falling like this, but I feel like I can't even have that, my own mistake, without having to take care of the family first." Her chin trembled and the tears came harder. "When will the family ever take care of me?"

She collapsed into the armchair under the weight of her sadness, the crushing realization that her family cared more for its hatred of one man than for her.

She flinched when her mother settled on the arm of the chair and touched her shoulder. "Diana, I love you. We all do. But we just—"

"Don't!" she cried, moving from under her mother's hand. "There's always a 'but' with you. Why is that?"

"Strength costs, Diana," her mother said. "But if you're strong, you can withstand anything. That's what I want for you—not the sadness that your father had. Not the sadness that I have."

"How can I be anything but sad when the only thing you've encouraged me to do was hate a stranger and give up my life for yours?" She took a sharp breath at the look on her mother's face. "I didn't mean that."

"Yes, you did." Her mother sighed. "I know you've done

a lot to keep the family on its feet since your father...left us. And it's gotten to be a habit for all of us to rely on you for so much. I should have stopped this before, but I admit we all got used to you being there no matter what." Her mother sighed. "Don't cry, baby." She lightly touched Diana's hair. "Please."

Diana looked up at her mother, drawing a deep breath. "I can't be strong like you want. I can only be myself."

Her mother opened her mouth, then closed it again. After a moment, she pressed her cool palms against Diana's cheeks, enveloping her in the scent of earth and the irises from her garden. "Then I'll be strong for you." She smoothed Diana's hair away from her face. "If Marcus Stanfield is what you want, open your heart to him. And if he's the man for you, he'll make his way to where he belongs."

Diana closed her eyes and nodded, feeling the last of her tears slip away.

Chapter 24

Marcus slept badly. He'd spent a restless night with sleep eluding him, and he'd been haunted by the traces of Diana's scent in his sheets and by the pain on her face when he admitted to buying up the land in Baltree Heights. But a result of his sleeplessness was a determination to win her back, to show her the canceled paperwork for the sale and ask her to allow him back into her life again.

At barely nine o'clock, he called his secretary.

"Good morning, Mr. Stanfield." Irene greeted him with her usual gentle efficiency, showing no surprise that he was calling her so early. The sound of her fingers steadily clacking away at the computer keys reached him through the phone.

"Good morning. Do you have the canceled contract for the Baltree Heights project on your desk? The courier was supposed to deliver it to you by this morning."

"Canceled contract?" The question in her voice made him freeze. "The contract wasn't canceled, sir. The money and deeds already changed hands, as of eight o'clock this morning."

"What?" He paused at the top of the stairs, the cell phone pressed to his ear. "Baltree is supposed to be dead in the water."

"Your father called shortly after you and I talked." Worry threaded through her voice. "He told me everything was proceeding forward as before. I thought it was fine since the lawyers already knew."

Marcus's hand tightened on the banister. "My father called you?"

"Yes. Is something wrong?"

He forced his teeth to unclench. "No. Nothing is wrong." He took a slow breath. "I won't be coming into the office after all. But you can reach me on my phone if you need anything."

"Of course, sir."

Marcus hung up the phone, wanting to hurl it against the wall. What had his father done? And why?

He left the house with only one destination in mind— his father's office. There, he politely pushed past his father's secretary until he was at the office door. He rapped quickly against the polished wood before stepping inside. His father was sitting at his desk, a slim middle-aged woman in a black suit perched across from him. They stopped in mid-conversation when Marcus walked in. His father took one look at his face before turning back to the woman.

"Let's continue the conversation another time, Maite."

The woman stood. "Of course, Quentin." Her voice, cool and well-modulated, held the touch of a Spanish accent.

Once the woman left, his father stood and walked from behind the desk, his face cautiously welcoming. The pale gray suit fit him well, emphasizing the aura of power he naturally wore.

"Good morning, Marcus. It's a surprise to see you on this side of the bridge so early."

"Why did you push the deal through after I told you it was canceled?"

His father gave him the hard-eyed stare Marcus had seen him level on his opponents across the boardroom.

"You were making a decision based on a woman's desires," his father said. "I looked into your Diana Hobbes and saw where she works. How often do I have to tell you never to make important decisions based on what a woman wants?"

Marcus winced, thinking then of his mother and how she had wanted the family to stay together, had wanted Cherish to stay close to home instead of being shipped off to boarding school abroad, but that hadn't mattered to his father. "My decision was already made. And it was *mine* to make."

"It was also mine to un-make." The look his father gave him was firm. Immovable.

"This is bull and you know it."

"Careful, son." His father's jaw hardened.

"I've been careful with you my entire life, and look where it's gotten me." He jerked his chin toward his father as the anger washed over him. "You don't even respect me enough to honor my business decisions."

"You earn respect. You don't get respect just because you're my son."

"And you don't get to disrespect me just because you're my father." He clenched his fist hard against his thigh. "It's done, Dad. No more. Let's break these ties of ours right here and now. If you can't treat me as an equal, then I see no use in us working together."

"Very well." His father's face was a stone wall. "If that's the decision you're going to make, then I'll stand by it." Some unnamed emotion moved across his face too quickly for Marcus to identify. "Now, if that's all, I have a meeting to get back to."

"Yes, get back to your meeting," Marcus spat. "Get back to screwing people over who have the misfortune of being in your path."

He turned without another word and left the office. An impotent anger toward his father and toward himself burned in his chest. What his father had done came as no surprise to him. Quentin Stanfield had always had a ruthless streak. He was just surprised at how badly it hurt when it was used against him. His father knew about Diana. He knew the hopes Marcus harbored regarding their budding relationship. But his father simply did not care.

He didn't want Diana to find out from anyone else. Marcus left his father's building and headed straight to her office. Minutes later, he found himself in her neighborhood, which would soon look nothing like it did now. All the tidy homes would be razed, and the grandmothers and grandfathers who'd been there for years would be forced out, a massive condo and strip mall of gourmet grocers and doggie day cares built in their midst. Marcus swallowed hard and rang the doorbell.

He didn't have to wait long.

"You don't have to ring the bell, you know." The young receptionist, Carla, greeted him with a welcoming smile. "You're here to see Diana, right?"

He nodded. "Right."

She pushed the door open to let him into the building that smelled of air-conditioning, warm paper and ink and fresh coffee.

"She's in with a family right now, but just give her a few minutes."

She indicated a small alcove nearby with a set of about seven chairs. Silver metal and functional. The kind he was used to seeing in casual dining restaurants in Miami and TV cop shows. He sank into one of the surprisingly comfortable chairs and waited.

Just like the last time he had been there during business hours, the office was a flurry of activity. The chime of the occasional phone ringing. Muffled echoes of conversations from another room. Somewhere, the distant ping of a microwave's bell. Not the breakneck pace of desperation, but the movement of a place where things were always being done because the work was such a pleasure. Guilt stabbed at him all over again.

He looked up when a couple walked out of the main office area and into the hallway with the receptionist. The woman held a child's hand, a boy who looked about eight years old, while her husband walked slightly ahead of them to open the front door for them to leave.

"Thank you again so much, Ms. Hobbes. We couldn't have done this without you."

Marcus's head jerked at the sound of Diana's last name. She walked behind the wife. Pretty and solemn in a pale yellow dress, a wide black belt around her waist, her hair in a tight bun. She looked professional but warm as she shook first the husband's hand, then kissed the wife and little boy on the cheek.

Once they were outside, she waved goodbye to the family and closed the door. Her faint smile decorated her mouth, although there was a certain tightness around her eyes. She turned to walk back to her office.

"Someone is here to see you, Diana." Carla delivered the news as if she were handing Diana a gift.

"Really? Who? I'm not expecting anyone else until after lunch."

The receptionist inclined her head in Marcus's direction. He stood up. Shoved a hand in his pocket. "Diana."

Her lips tightened. "Marcus." She nodded her thanks at the receptionist, then looked at him. He saw the struggle on her face. To talk to him or not. To throw him out of her space or be adult about this. "What brings you here?" she asked.

"Something important that I want to discuss with you." His fingers clenched and released around the keys in his pocket.

"Come to my office," she grudgingly said.

He followed her and closed the door behind him. In the middle of the room, she paused, glancing between her desk and the couch. Finally, she made a decision and sat on the couch. She crossed her legs as he took a seat next to her. "Thank you again for not going through with the land purchase. I really appreciate that. Instead of using our recent donations to move, we can use them to expand our services like we've been talking about for years." A light of excitement flickered in her eyes. She glanced at him, a tentative look, inviting him to share her pleasure.

He winced. "About that..."

There was no way to soften the blow and make himself look like any less of a fool or coward. "The deal. It went through."

She leaned back from him. "What?"

"I tried to stop it, but I was too late. My father pushed the deal through."

He saw the shock come over her face. The realization of what that meant.

"But you told me you were going to take care of it," she said.

"I'm sorry."

Her warmth in the sofa beside him suddenly became stone-cold. "I had a suspicion you wouldn't allow yourself to lose money on this. You're a businessman before anything else. I shouldn't have let myself believe you'd let money slip through your fingers just because I asked you to." She pressed her lips together, lashes fluttering in agitation. A hand clenched into the edge of the sofa, the knuckles turning gray. "Please leave."

The pain in her eyes slayed him. "Diana, I tried to make this go away."

"Now you can do the next best thing and make yourself go away." She abruptly stood up and backed away from him. Her gaze speared down at him. "I'm sure you won't mind that I don't see you out."

Marcus was used to volatile women who threw things. Who yelled and screamed in the throes of their anger. Diana was frozen. An icicle straight to his chest.

"You have to believe I did everything I could," he said.

"Obviously you didn't. Please. I'm finished with this conversation." She turned her back to him and walked to her desk. "Just leave my office. Leave this building. I think you've done enough for us."

His whole body groaned with regret as he levered himself up from the couch. "For what it's worth, I really am sorry about this."

"It's not worth the dirt under your shoe." She sat in the chair behind her desk.

He watched her, feeling bereft. Angry at himself for allowing things to go this far when he could have taken care of it all before the fund-raiser at his house. Now he had lost her. And lost the regard he once had for his father. Marcus turned to leave.

"Tell me."

He paused at the sound of her voice.

"Why did you fix our porch and do all these things for us if you planned on demolishing the building anyway?" Cold voice. Granite eyes. Hands flat against the top of her desk. Unmoving. As if more hinged on his answer than he would ever imagine.

He didn't bother denying that he had been the anonymous donor who sent the contractor over to fix the hurricane damage. "I did it because I wanted to make you happy."

A bitter smile stretched the corners of her mouth. "I guess you're no longer interested in making me happy."

Before he could reply, she looked down at her computer and tapped the keyboard, effectively dismissing him. Marcus's chest felt encased in ice, his body numb and cold from her complete dismissal. He wanted to say more. He wanted to get her to look at him again. He wanted the world.

But she only tapped at the computer keys as if he was no longer standing there. As if he didn't exist. Feeling loss like he'd never known before, he turned and left her office. As he walked through the narrow hallway and toward the door, he felt the eyes of Diana's colleagues on him. He forced himself to walk at the same pace when he wanted to rush away from their looks of condemnation.

"That was a short visit," Carla chirped as he approached the vestibule.

He smiled tightly. "Every good thing must come to an end." He tapped fingers to his forehead in a casual salute. "See you some other time."

"Have a good afternoon!" She smiled back.

Out on the street, he stood still for a moment, watching the light traffic wind past his car. Young men stood on the street corner. A woman pushed a stroller while a boy skipped at her side. A grandmother sat on her porch listening to gospel music on the radio at her side.

All this was changing. Because of him.

He drew in a breath and pushed it out. He tried to think like his father in that moment—no regrets—but couldn't. Marcus sighed again, then got in his car and drove away.

Chapter 25

Diana wasn't sure she wanted to go to Bailey and Seven Carmichael's party. It had been weeks since she and Marcus had talked. Since that disastrous morning he had come to see her in her office. Her office that was now packing up in preparation to move to a higher-rent office miles away from her house and from the city.

She hadn't done much socializing, either personally or for Building Bridges, afraid that she would run into Marcus. Diana had spent nearly nine weeks keeping mostly to herself, going on occasional spa dates with Trish, rebuilding her relationship with Jason and spending more time with her mother.

She'd tried to allow the truth of her mother's words to manifest itself. That if Marcus belonged with her, he would make his way back. But in these past two months, she hadn't seen or heard from him. The pain of his absence had brought her to tears on many nights, leaving her sobbing in bed, unable to catch her breath.

Still, despite the way things had ended between them, whenever she remembered Marcus, she remembered how good it felt to be with someone who didn't demand, who only gave and loved and cherished her and made her feel more desirable than she ever had in her life. But she had to get over that. She had to allow those memories to fade and lose their power over her.

It was Bailey Carmichael who pulled her out of her funk. Her new friend had come to her office with cupcakes to share the news that she was pregnant. She wanted Diana to come to the baby shower. But before that shower, she wanted to throw a party.

Glowing in a white pantsuit that fit her still-slender frame perfectly, Bailey told Diana she would love to have her over.

"But I don't want to run into…anyone," Diana said.

"You won't. I haven't seen Marcus in ages. I think he's out of the country. Seven knows for sure, but I haven't asked him."

And so Diana agreed to go to the party, and she brought Trish with her as her plus one. The party was a lavish affair in the penthouse apartment Seven had recently acquired through a bizarre trade for a sculpture from a businessman in Dubai. The apartment was even grander than the one they already owned. It was on the bay, overlooking the glittering lights of downtown. Stepping out on the balcony of the fiftieth-floor apartment made it seem entirely possible to touch the stars.

Diana stood on the balcony, looking up at the sky. And wishing. She had a drink in her hand, something sweet and frothy Seven had given her with a gentle smile. Diana had nodded her thanks, knowing he probably thought she was pathetic for still pining over Marcus. A man who had broken the simplest of promises to her. Promises he hadn't even had to make. She tasted the drink, swallowed the sour and sweet concoction and sighed.

"Stop blowing all that air over there. You're making my chest hurt."

Trish walked onto the balcony carrying a glass of champagne, always her drink of choice. She wore a clinging red dress, her new waist-length hair draped over her breast as she slid the door closed and joined Diana under the stars.

"I can do what I want," Diana said petulantly.

"It's my party and I'll cry if I want to?"

Diana made a sound that could have been a laugh. "It's Bailey's party, you know."

"Hmm. I'm sure you've done enough crying for both of you." Trish came to stand beside her. The smell of her perfume surrounded Diana with its sticky sweetness. Her friend rested her arms against the railing and leaned over to look down. The crystal-blue pool. The bay. Other apartments. Beautiful Miami. "Why don't you at least try to find Marcus?" At Diana's poisonous look, she threw up her hands, sipped her champagne. "Or you could at least try dating again. I know you got used to that good sex with him. Find a replacement. Live your life."

If only it were that easy. She'd never met a man as generous in bed, as funny, as easy to be with as Marcus. Every time she heard Johnny Hartman sing, she thought of him. Every time she imagined stepping out of her day-to-day routine, she imagined doing it with him.

The week before, she'd taken off an impromptu weekend and flown to a small mountain town in Mexico with beautiful doors and bougainvillea draped throughout the landscape. She went alone, spoke the decent amount of Spanish she'd learned from living in Miami and surprised herself by having a good time. She'd thought of him, imagined him, watched the sunrise and wanted him by her side.

She wouldn't have gone if she hadn't known Marcus. He made stepping outside of her comfort zone seem so easy. And it *had* been easy. All she had to do was buy the ticket and arrange for her temporary rooftop casa, and that had been that.

"I wish I could do that, Trish. I really do."

Her friend pursed her lips. "Well, the least you can do, then, is come inside to this party with me and enjoy yourself instead of standing out here and moping. The music is great, the champagne is divine, and every hot body in there is gorgeous enough to make me think of going bisexual."

Diana chuckled weakly. "Really, Trish?"

"Come on. You're not getting any younger, and you're not going to get laid by standing out here alone."

"But I don't want to get laid."

"Ha! You say that now, but wait until you see the thick and tender meat that walked in while you were out here doing your solo Romeo and Juliet act."

"What?"

"Come on." Trish tossed back the last of her champagne and tucked her arm through Diana's. "The night is young, and you're too beautiful not to share it with a hot and hung stud."

She opened the balcony door, and the sounds of the latest hit song by Beyoncé poured out over them. Trish was right. The party was lively, and just about everyone was gorgeous. She recognized a few people from the dinner parties she'd attended at Bailey and Seven's place in the past. Many were artist types with interesting hair and beautifully patterned and bright dresses.

"See what I mean?" Trish squeezed her hand and jerked her chin toward the room full of hotness.

Diana had to smile. With a carefree smile, Trish tugged her toward a circle of people gathered not far from the door—three impressive-looking men and two women. Diana could already see how Trish's mind was working.

The five-some glanced their way as they joined them, the men bowled over by Trish as usual, the women giving both her and Diana interested smiles.

"We want in on this conversation," Trish said with a laugh as they walked up.

One of the women laughed, too, looking Trish over with more than platonic interest. "Come on in, beautiful ladies. There's always room for more."

The others apparently agreed because in moments, they absorbed Diana and Trish into their discussion about the cliquish nature of the Miami art scene.

"What do you think?" one of the men who'd introduced himself as Alfonso asked. His brown eyes were warm and familiar as he checked out Diana's body.

Although she wasn't by any means interested in him, she was glad she'd made an effort and put on the vintage Dior, a pale pink dress that hugged her torso and flared out around her knees, emphasizing her curves and down-playing the weight she'd lost in recent weeks.

"I don't know much about the art scene here, I'm afraid," she said with a shrug. "I work in nonprofit."

"Oh, really? I'd love to show you around and show you what I like." Alfonso's smile was even warmer now. "And of course, you can tell me all about your work."

Trish directed a Cheshire cat grin at her, although her friend seemed to be busy negotiating something with the woman who had called her beautiful.

"That would be nice," Diana said. "I love—" Her voice trailed off as familiar wide shoulders caught her eye. The rest of her words dropped back down her throat. She swallowed. Looked again, but the shoulders had disappeared.

No. It couldn't be him. Bailey said he was out of the country.

"Are you okay?" Alfonso asked the question the same moment Trish touched her back in concern.

"Honey?"

Diana shook herself. "Oh…I'm fine. I just thought I saw someone I knew."

Trish's expression cleared. She looked up and around the room, eyes narrowed. Diana cleared her throat and refocused on Alfonso. "I'm sorry. What was I saying?"

A quick smile flashed across the man's face. "You were saying you'd love to go out with me to Miami Art Walk tomorrow evening."

Diana curled her cold fingers into the hem of her dress and tried to match his expression. "That would be—"

"She'll be busy tomorrow night."

The entire circle turned to see who had spoken. But Diana didn't need to look. Her mouth silently formed his name. Not in surprise, but relief. She realized then that she had been waiting for him. Ever since she'd arrived at the party. Ever since he'd walked out of her office all those weeks ago. She had been waiting.

"Listen, man—"

But Trish put a hand on Alonso's arm and shook her head. A warm hand touched Diana's back, burning into her skin through the dress. She smelled him, like the breeze of the ocean. Marcus.

She turned. "I don't want to talk to you."

Or at least that was what she started to say. But the sight of him stopped her. His cheekbones were more pronounced than when she'd seen him last. But he looked incredible in a dark vest buttoned over a plaid, long-sleeved shirt rolled up to reveal muscular arms, faded jeans with a wide leather belt that emphasized the masculine heaviness of his crotch, and leather boots. Delicious. She felt like a woman lost in the desert for days suddenly faced with an oasis. A fountain. Green palm trees overhead. Water to slake her long and undeniable thirst.

She flinched away from him, unable to bear the way her body melted and tingled at his touch. Hurt flickered in his eyes but made him seem more determined that ever to say what he came to.

"Step outside with me for a minute?" He watched her as if nothing else in the world mattered.

Diana felt the interested eyes of the others in the circle on her, on Marcus. Their curiosity. Even Alfonso was staring from her to Marcus with fascination.

"I have nothing to say to you, Marcus." *It's been over two months,* she wanted to scream at him. Two months where part of her had hoped he would come back and try again, say something else to her. "I—"

Trish squeezed her hand. "Why don't you go somewhere more private, honey?" Her best friend's words were soft, a gentle warning in her ear.

It was only then Diana realized that it wasn't just the circle that stared at her and Marcus. Almost the entire room had grown quiet to watch and see what would be the outcome of this unexpected drama. Hot color rushed under her cheeks.

"No," she said. And the word was loud. Louder than she'd intended. And those who hadn't been looking at them freely stared now.

Marcus only watched her with infinite patience. His body was still and quiet, as if he would wait for her until the end of time.

"You'll regret it if you don't," Trish said softly.

And suddenly, Diana knew her friend was right. She had been waiting for Marcus, and now he was here. Had

she been waiting only to turn him away? Or was this her
chance to release the sadness that had lingered around her
life like stale perfume?

Diana walked away from the circle of eyes and went out
toward the balcony. Marcus followed silently, then stepped
easily in front of her to open the sliding glass door. The
door whispered closed behind her as he pulled it shut.
She was more than aware of the clear glass and the eyes
still on them, but she thought of the dangers of being in a
private room away from the others, the strong possibility
that he would use her weakness against her and she would
end up on her knees, her love for him a thudding heartbeat
against her tongue.

But was this worse?

He turned to look at her. A beautiful man. A man beyond compare.

"I've wanted to see you for weeks." His voice was
rough. In need.

"I didn't want to see you," she lied.

He shoved his hands in his pockets. She watched his
fists clench through the thick material of his jeans. "Diana.
I never wanted things to be like this. My—I made a mis-
calculation." He clenched his teeth, as if trying to prevent
himself from saying something terrible. "I shouldn't have
gone into business with my father." Marcus shook his head.
"That partnership is over now."

She felt a hitch in her throat. Was that the truth? Or
was he saying whatever he needed to get back into her
bed? But even as the question tripped through her mind,
she realized he had never lied to her. He'd left things out,
but he'd never lied.

"My father is not a bad man," Marcus said. "He—"

Diana clenched her back teeth. She hadn't come out to
the balcony to talk about Quentin Stanfield. She already

knew where she stood with him. "What is it that you have to say to me, Marcus? I have to get back to the party."

"You mean get back to that prick with the goatee who probably couldn't get it up enough to satisfy you?" His face became hard then, its naked jealousy a dangerous and exhilarating thing.

"Yes." She propped her fists on her hips, challenging him with her gaze.

His face spasmed in pain. Her breath caught. "Don't do that," he said. Voice tortured. Pain naked. His hands left his pockets. "Please don't."

She swallowed. "Why not?"

"Because even though I messed up, I love you." He blew out a harsh breath. "You have to know that."

She didn't. How could she? "You only want me in your bed. That's all you've ever wanted. And you kept things from me to keep me there."

"That's not true. I was going to tell you about the deal, but I was too afraid of your reaction. I was afraid of *this*. Forgive me, please." He dropped to one knee and she gasped, a hand flying to her mouth. "I need you, Diana." His other knee met the ground. "I've been a wreck over this for weeks."

God help her, she wanted this. She wanted *him*. But what would she become if she ignored what he had done?

"Marcus…" She shook her head. "Please get up."

He stayed at her feet. "You can have the land where the center is. I've bought it back from my father. I won't undo my plans for the community, but you can stay in the building rent free. Even if you don't come back to me, you can have it. On my life, I never meant for any of this to hurt you."

"But I *was* hurt," she said, her chin wobbling with the onset of tears.

But those hurts were melting away until all she could feel was the love running through her, overflowing her eyes and running down her face. Her knees buckled until she was on the ground with him, their bodies close, his pain a mirror of hers.

"Do you forgive me?"

"I—" She shook her head, trying to clear her mind and separate the euphoria of seeing him from the agony of the past two months.

Diana swallowed thickly as she choked on the betrayal she had felt when he kept the secret of Baltree Heights from her. When she had trusted him so implicitly. When she was willing to risk her family's anger and disappointment to be with him.

She clawed at her own throat. "I'm not sure if I can trust you again," she finally said. "My mother. My brother. It was like you proved them right. And I felt like a fool for being taken in by you like that."

"Diana, you have no idea how much I regret what happened. I'm so damn sorry." Marcus gripped her waist, his gold eyes dark and tortured. "I'll do anything to fix it. I'll talk with Jason and your mother. I'll take a polygraph." His hands tightened even more in desperation. "Whatever you or they need me to do, I will do it. I was being stupid before. Just say you'll forgive me and come back into my life."

Even more tears burned Diana's eyes at his passionate words. How could she say no to him? How could she say no to their love?

"Yes," she said. "Yes, I do. I will." Because the pain of the past few weeks without him was something she never wanted to feel again.

"Thank God!" He hugged her close, and she fell into his arms.

He pressed kisses to her cheeks, her forehead, her mouth. He tasted like her tears. His body was firm and warm and familiar and so deeply missed. Diana opened her mouth under his, pulling his beloved flavor into her, savoring him with her tongue, her hands pressed against his belly through the vest and shirt.

The heat of the familiar desire flooded her and she sighed, fingers sinking deeply into the cotton over his muscled stomach. She vaguely heard the whisper of motion, the sliding of a heavy door over gliders. Someone cleared their throat.

She and Marcus pulled away from each other to see Trish in the balcony's doorway. "I think you better take the lovefest someplace more private, unless you want to give us all a show." Trish grinned at them, then disappeared back inside.

Embarrassment flooded Diana's cheeks, and she buried her face in Marcus's chest in mortification. "Oh, my God!" Caught up in the feeling of rightness that had taken her over, she'd completely forgotten about their audience. Marcus's laughter vibrated under her cheek.

He touched the back of her neck, his laughter fading. "I don't care who's watching, as long as you're with me."

Diana smiled widely and lifted her face to look at him.

"You want to get out of here, love?" His voice was low with sensual promise.

She nodded. His lips touched her forehead and he pulled away, then stood. Then he held out his hand to help her to her feet. Diana took it and rose up into his arms, tumbling once and always into the warmth of his smile.

Epilogue

"Are you sure you're ready to do this?" Seven raised a teasing eyebrow as he walked into the church's vestry that smelled of candle wax and cut flowers.

Marcus wasn't in the mood for teasing. He was nervous as hell. He adjusted his black silk tie one last time in the mirror before turning to look at his best man. Seven was more than presentable in his tailored black suit with its lavender silk tie the same shade as the bridesmaids' dresses.

"Of course I'm ready," he said.

But he couldn't deny the tremor in his hands. He'd never been so nervous about anything in his life. Business deals. Confronting his father about his duplicity. Losing his virginity. None of those things had prepared him for this feeling that was part vulnerability, part pride, part "are you sure you know what you're doing?"

Diana, the woman he loved, was waiting somewhere out there for him in the Catholic church his family had worshipped in for generations. It was a big day for them both—a proud day. There was only one thing threatening to mess it up.

"Is her mother here yet?" He cracked his knuckles, blowing out a steadying breath.

Seven shook his head and looked at his watch. "But we don't start the music for another fifteen minutes or so."

Marcus winced. Although they had had their own share of problems, it meant a lot to Diana that her mother finally supported the relationship she had with Marcus. It also meant a lot to his fiancée that her mother was there at the wedding.

Marcus's own mother got along so well with Diana that the two of them, along with Trish, had tackled the details of the wedding like the most important mission of their lives. Cheryl Hobbes-Freeman had shown little interest in being part of the planning, had even declined being in the wedding party, but she said she would be there in the audience to support her daughter.

Everyone was under the impression that she was coming, but fifteen minutes until the start of the ceremony, there was still no sign of her. Frowning, Marcus sent Trish a quick text and hoped that Diana's best friend would come through.

"We've all done what we can." Marcus rolled his shoulders to loosen them up. He was sweating. His pulse was doing the tango in his throat. In the mirror, he managed to look calm, even like bridegroom material in the three-piece midnight-black suit. He touched the yellow rosebud in his lapel and thought of Diana. He was ready. "Let's go."

Just then, a brisk knock sounded. The door opened. "You're not trying to run out on my sister, are you?"

Jason stood in the doorway dressed in his groomsman's suit, his quick gaze taking in the contents of the vestry and the two men who stood together in front of the mirror. The room looked as if a small hurricane had torn though it, a result of Marcus's earlier nervousness after his father left to make sure everything was running smoothly downstairs in the church.

He and Quentin Stanfield were still having a few problems, fallout from what his father had tried to do with the Baltree Heights property. But in the end, Quentin was his father and had come to him with congratulations, a ridiculously expensive gift for the bride and the insistence on paying for every bit of the wedding.

Diana had been reluctant to accept his (to her) suspicious generosity, and Marcus respected whatever choice she made regarding his father. But Quentin and Diana had had a private conversation a few days before the wedding that had seemingly settled everything between them. Marcus hadn't asked about the details of the conversation. It was enough that Diana was content. He shook himself back to the present.

"Running is not something I do," Marcus said in response to Jason's earlier comment. "I'm ready for this."

The younger man tightened his jaw and gave a look that Marcus was coming to learn was reluctant respect. "Let's go, then. It's almost showtime."

With Seven at his side, Marcus turned to leave the vestry when Jason stopped short. "What are you doing here?" he asked in surprise. "Marcus is right behind me."

Marcus stepped from behind the younger man to see a flash of white silk chiffon disappear into a nearby doorway. He heard Diana's low voice.

"Mother isn't here." A hint of her rosemary perfume reached him, making him smile.

"You know it's bad luck to see the groom before the wedding," Jason said. "And you two need all the luck you can get."

His rough protection of Diana, something that had grated on Marcus's nerves in the beginning, actually warmed him now. The boy was just trying to look after his sister, since there had been no one else to do it for so long. But now Marcus was here, too.

"I don't believe in luck," Marcus said. But he stayed behind Jason anyway, knowing that despite whatever had brought Diana upstairs to seek him out, she did believe in that small tradition. He was grateful when Seven stepped up to also block his view. Marcus called out to Diana. "Don't worry, love. Your mother will be here soon."

Her soft voice, threaded with anxiety, floated to him through the hallway. "Are you sure?"

"Of course. I won't allow anything to ruin this day for you."

That hint of white chiffon in the hallway shifted. He could practically hear her mind working, worrying and planning her next move. He shook his head and smiled. Brilliant women and their machinations. "Go get ready for your wedding, Ms. Hobbes. It's almost time for you to make your entrance." And it was time for him to be standing next to the priest, pledging his life to her. "Just for you, everything will be perfect."

After a moment, he heard her dress rustling again. Then a sigh. "Okay. Turn around," she said.

Marcus grinned and turned his back to her.

"Are you looking?" Her voice quavered.

Jason made a disgusted noise.

"Not at all."

Marcus closed his eyes when he heard her dress brushing the ground as she dashed through the hallway, her footsteps quiet as if she wasn't wearing any shoes. He breathed in the faint scent of her perfume again, hints of rosemary and honey, a new body oil she'd started wearing in the past six months. It did something to him every morning to wake up to the sweet and lingering smell of her in his sheets and pillows long after she'd gone.

"Okay. She left." Jason's dress shoes rapped against the stone floors as he started off after his sister.

Seven patted his back once. An urgent gesture. "Let's go."

Marcus didn't need to be told twice. As they got to the top of the stairs, his cell phone chirped with a new message. He looked down at it and smiled in satisfaction. Today was definitely going to be a good day. He quickened his footsteps.

Downstairs in the church, the groomsmen were greeting the last of the guests and making sure that they got to the correct side of the aisle, to the correct chair, and, in the case of a few of the elderly attendants, that they were at the correct church.

The building was packed with people from both families, friends, acquaintances and a few reporters granted access to the wedding. At first, Marcus had declined all media requests, but Trish had teased him about being too damn selfish, telling him that maybe one day Diana would like to look at some of the local magazines and see her dress and big day featured inside their pages. So Marcus had given in.

He made his way from the side stairs to the front of the church, conscious of the many eyes on him. The woolly-haired priest was already waiting for him at the altar in his flowing white vestments, his kind brown hands clasped in front of him as he took in the attendees and then Marcus.

"Are you doing well, my son?" The priest's dark eyes sought out Marcus.

He took a deep breath. "Yes, Father. I am."

"Very good."

Seven settled into his place at Marcus's side. He patted the pocket of his vest, probably to make sure the rings
were still there, then squeezed Marcus's shoulder. "Are you
absolutely sure you're ready for this?" His eyes glittered
with merciless humor. He knew that Marcus had waited a
long time for this moment.

"I think I've been ready since the moment I met Diana,"
he said.

But that didn't stop his heart from machine-gunning
in his chest. To help calm down, he searched the church
for his family and friends, most of whom had thought this
day would never come.

His father sat in the front row next to his mother, both
of them apparently trying very hard not to look at each
other. His stepmother sat on the other side of her husband,
but stared daggers at the former Mrs. Quentin Stanfield.
Marcus's mother looked unfazed.

At the back of the church, the last of the groomsmen
trickled outside to pair up with the bridesmaids and get
ready to escort them down the aisle. Marcus forced himself
not to look at his watch again. He swallowed as the doors
fell closed, cutting off all natural light in the church except
for the sun pouring in rich shades of aquamarine, scarlet
and gold through the stained glass skylights and windows.

"Okay," Seven said to the priest. "I think we're ready."

But just as everyone settled into place, the double doors
opened again. A blade of bright sunshine swept through
the church, illuminating the sea of people inside it. An
older couple walked in.

"Oh! Excuse me," a woman said softly.

She came into the church wearing a plain but beautiful blue lace dress. The look on her face was harried, but
she and her escort walked in with a quiet dignity. Marcus
caught a glimpse of Trish just outside the church doors.

Diana's best friend watched the couple for a moment to make sure they were taken care of, then she closed the double doors once again.

Marcus looked at Seven, and his friend immediately took charge. He quietly rushed down the aisle to usher the woman and her husband to the front of the church and to the bride's side. Marcus released a breath he hadn't even realized he had been holding. Now the wedding could begin.

He turned to the priest, who smiled benignly before nodding toward the orchestra for them to play the processional music. Tension dropped into Marcus's chest again. He swallowed thickly as the church's front doors were pulled open once again to the low and haunting sounds of the piano.

Marcus tightened and released his fists at his sides as the wedding party made its way down the aisle. The groomsmen and bridesmaids were paired up and seemed to walk forever. Then came Trish, the maid of honor. Finally, the music changed to "Here Comes the Bride." Two flower girls in yellow dresses walked in side by side, dropping yellow rose petals as they went.

Marcus's breath nearly left him.

Escorted by her brother, Diana walked down the aisle toward him in a dress that he would probably never remember after that day. All he saw was her face. Her breathtaking beauty and trembling smile. Her hair was pinned up under a floral tiara, and a veil framed the loveliness of the woman he'd fallen completely in love with.

With her face uncovered, he was able to see her every emotion. Her anxiety. The love in her eyes when she saw him. He also knew the exact moment when she noticed her mother at the front of the church. Her footsteps faltered for a moment. Her chin wobbled. Then she straight-

ened her posture and glided toward him on the carpet of
yellow roses.

Jason escorted her to Marcus's side, then placed her
hand in his.

"Take care of her," he growled.

But the boy wasn't telling Marcus anything that he
didn't already plan on doing.

"Chill," he said to Jason.

Then he was done giving his attention where it did not
belong. Diana's fingers grasped his.

"Thank you," she said as a single tear fell down her
cheek. "Thank you for making sure my mother got here."

He squeezed her hand in return. "Did you doubt me?"

She blushed and briefly looked away, then smiled. "Not
you," she said. "Her."

But her mother had made it there anyway, despite a flat
tire and not having a spare in the trunk and being unable to
reach Diana to tell her that she and her husband were having troubles. Luckily, Diana's mother had finally thought to
call Trish, and the day had been saved. Diana's special day.

"I love you," she whispered for his ears alone. "So very,
very much."

As the priest faced the congregation and the music sub-
sided, all the love Marcus felt for Diana rose over him like
a warm and all-encompassing wave. He gratefully surrendered to it.

"I love you, Diana." His voice deepened. "For always."

* * * * *

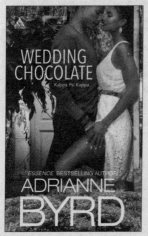

REQUEST YOUR FREE BOOKS!

2 FREE NOVELS PLUS 2 FREE GIFTS!

KIMANI™
ROMANCE

Love's ultimate destination!

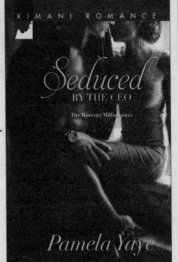